The Movement

A Prodigy's Encounter with the Music of Heaven

May you encounter the love of the Father,

By

Chris Cochand

Chris Cochand

The Movement:
A Prodigy's Encounter with the Music of Heaven
Copyright © 2020 by Chris Cochand

Published by DREAM Publishing & Design.
info@dreampublishing.ca

Dedication

This book is dedicated to my bride and my four beautiful children. You are the greatest accompaniment to heaven's song in my life.

In loving memory of Jason Racz. I never knew I could write until I had to find the words to say goodbye and comfort the ones you left behind.

Table of Contents

Acknowledgments and Thanks

I'm not religious. Yet you won't get far before discovering that God is one of the main characters in this book. From the beginning of time religion has attempted to define deity through fashioned form, sacred ritual and the pursuit of piety. Organized religion is like a message in a bottle trying to describe the ocean with words like 'big,' 'blue' and 'deep'. All the while floating safely on its surface untouched by its salty spray, hoping to reach the masses with its message when all one needs to do is dive in and venture deep. This isn't meant as a stab at religion. If anything it highlights how vast, deep, and endless the ocean of God really is. I want my life to be defined by my pursuit of the deepest depths of the heart of God, which is the farthest thing from a religious exercise. It's a life-changing encounter every day of which he is the initiator.

God has been trying to get our attention since the beginning of creation, revealing himself through aha moments as simple as a kiss or as substantial as the cosmos. He is constantly in pursuit of us, trying to break through our preconceived ideas and say here I am. This story is just another one of those moments where he comes along to break the bottle floating on the surface, saturating it in overwhelming waves of grace. He's actually disrupted a lot to tell this story. You see, there's something else you should probably know: I've never written anything before. Before this story started I never wrote any more than a post on social media or a poem in high school. I wrote papers in college, but they were nothing more than a means to an end with no connection to the heart. Then one day I found myself interrupted by God's whimsical sense of humor, when he dropped this story along my path provoking a momentous collision between my head and my heart. I never sat down and said to myself, I think I'm going to write a story — let alone a novel!

Someone once told me twenty years ago that he saw me writing books one day, but I figured that this was just indigestion having its way with a man whose word I otherwise deeply respected. But, as involuntary as a heartbeat, this story one day suddenly awoke with a pulse of its own.

It was December 2017, late in the evening, and I was driving to the hospital where my wife worked, to drop something off. As I drove, I became aware of this story being deposited into my mind, like boxes filling an empty room from floor to ceiling. It felt as though my imagination was taking a trip without my permission and as I drove, all the characters, along with the plot from climax to completion, were being laid out before me. I would have dismissed this as a random experience, but couldn't shake the compulsion that followed to write it all down. I wrote the outline and then tried to write the story a few times—by then I thought maybe my friend's word was slightly more than indigestion? But I struggled with writer's block and felt like I was trying to light a damp firecracker in the rain. Writing is hard. Life is busy. The story was shelved. Little did I know the wick had lit but would smolder for almost two years before finally igniting.

I wouldn't have started writing again if it had not been for Jason and Kris Vallotton and their first Born Wild Men's Retreat in May 2019, held at a picturesque ranch in the heartland of Texas. If Jason had not responded to my unconventional petition with grace, and if Kris had not told me to "write!" this story would not have been told. This book is written with my thanks to these beautiful men who have been faithful to God's call in their lives.

The Movement

Part I

Prologue

Michael Mann was different. It's not like his mother tried to raise him differently. She heard of some parents enveloping their children with music while still in the womb or serenading them to sleep with a nocturne in the night, willing them to absorb "the gift" through osmosis. Helen Mann didn't always have music on in the background as some of her closest friends were known to do. Music was just there like scenery, an ever changing landscape she didn't have time to stop for as she rushed to her next destination in life. But Michael noticed. He was not only captivated by every rhythm and note, it was inside him, always looking for a way to break out like a penned wild mustang testing the fences.

He was the first boy among the Mann children, which complicated matters when Helen first started to notice the subtle differences. The toys and games which entertained Michael's three older sisters through their early years of life held no value in his eyes. When the dump trucks and dragons began to arrive, Michael would stare through them as though regarding ethereal shadows wandering the playroom in search for their lost purpose and soul. Besides, he was on a search of his own.

Blustery days brought a set of wind chimes on the front porch to life, and pulled Michael to the window from wherever he was in the house to stare in fixated stillness. Outside, he would stare at the trees as though their rhythmic sway held the interpretation to the mysteries of life. There were no instruments in the Mann house. How were his parents to know music was the language of his soul?

The first time Michael approached a piano, he had just turned three years old. It would be an encounter that would change his life. Miss Anne's School for ballet was nothing special for a venue. Miss Anne had leased the space above the local barber shop for the past thirteen years in an aging two-story building built over fifty years ago. It was located in the old part of Marysville in Washington State. There was also, of course, the Marysville School of Music and Dance and the Take 5 Dance Academy by the high school, which attracted more of the upper class and aspiring dancers of Marysville because the buildings were modern and the instructors well accomplished. But the Mann family had been taking their three daughters to Miss Anne for the past two years because, above all, she was kind in her approach and spoke encouragement into the lives of her students venturing well beyond the regimen of curriculum.

Miss Anne's solid wood floors were tired and showed their age. The fact that they were polished did nothing to mask the sound of creaks and groans under the weight of fluttering, fumbling, and stomping from little children's feet. A vibrant cacophony vied for attention against the local country radio station and conversation in Mr. Tucker's barber shop in the space below. Fortunately for Miss Anne, Mr. Tucker and most of his retired clients didn't mind the mix of clamor and country.

Miss Anne kept the piano in her studio, strategically positioned in the corner along the back wall of the stairway where the floorboards were prone to make the most noise. It was Matt's turn to take the Mann kids: eight-year-old twins Faith and Felicity, Madeline their six-year-old sister, and Michael the three-year-old boy, to dance lessons. Helen taught at Marysville High School and had to stay late to mark mid-term assignments.

It had been a typical day in the Mann family so far. Matt was a

12

captain in the Marysville Fire Department and had woken at two that afternoon after sleeping off a night shift. He had picked up Michael from daycare and the girls from school. They'd arrived at Miss Anne's with enough time for the girls to stretch and change before their class started promptly at four. Normally, Matt would take Michael across the street to the park in the square to keep him occupied and out of trouble. But because Michael had fallen asleep in the car on the drive over, Matt had him sitting on his knees, slowly waking up on a bench along the wall with the rest of the watching parents. When the piano started to play, Michael was awake — as though for the first time.

The girls were thrilled to be dancing in front of their daddy, which made it hard for them to concentrate through the lesson. At the end of class, Miss Anne had all of her students sitting in a circle where she took the time to individually acknowledge the good job and strengths she saw in each one of them that day. While things were wrapping up, Michael quietly slipped down from his dad's lap and approached the piano, which had captivated him through the entire lesson while the dancers responded to the sounds and melodies it made.

Most boys of Michael's age, if given the chance to sit before the keys of a piano, would smash at them like it was a whack-a-mole game. But not Michael. One key at a time, he began to gently push down and pause long enough to absorb the sound before moving on to the next key. Michael was looking for something. Like a boy staring out into a massive pile of Lego blocks amassed across the living room floor, he was lost in complete concentration while he searched for the missing piece. And perhaps the reason why Matt didn't bound up immediately to intervene in the interruption was because the sound Michael made was gentle and methodical — and nobody really took notice.

And then Michael found his note. It would be the sound that burst a dam in his little heart and introduced purpose to his poise on the piano bench. If anyone had been watching closely — really closely — they would have seen the hairs standing up on the back of his neck and a spark flash in his eyes. The moment passed, but he continued to search for more sounds he knew lay trapped behind the black and white ivory bricks. He had heard Miss Anne playing a song that day, while sitting at this same instrument, this vehicle of sound, and didn't want to stop until he could turn the key and make its engine hum again.

Matt and the other parents glanced over at Michael a few times while he intently carried on. Miss Anne looked up with a smile from her circle a few times — probably just relieved the boy wasn't being completely obnoxious.

"Better put him in lessons Matt. He's pretty good for a three-year-old," a parent inserted with light laughter. A crowd started to gather around the piano as the class wrapped up and children started to leave the circle. It was hard not to stare at this little boy going up and down the keys with methodical determination. People were starting to notice that much at least as he continued to plunk at the keys. More light hearted laughter at the odd comment or joke grew as the entire class and parents started to circle around. Michael didn't notice any of them. And then it happened. A familiar tune in its most rudimentary form began to rise up out of the oak and ivory at the hands of a child, who just hours ago, raged because he couldn't have an apple juice box in the car.

"Sweet Jesus," one parent said at a whisper as though a single breath would topple the masterpiece manifesting before them like fresh gossamer unwoven in a whirlwind. The sound of the piano was now the only thing heard in the room as all other activity fell to a pregnant hush. Miss Anne was a sudden quiver of goosebumps and moist eyes as the tune became more polished and clear with every meticulous and calculated refrain at the small child's hands. One of the students started to dance and move quietly on the floor as a familiar melody they had danced to earlier started to resonate once again within the walls of the studio. The tune was the Swan Lake theme by Tchaikovsky. And now, as though heaven itself invited Miss Anne's School of Ballet to dance to the sound of a miracle, Michael Mann, at three years old, was playing that same song.

I am Michael Mann, and this is my story.

Chapter 1: The Trees Are Singing

The first memories of a child are a curious phenomenon. Though a child has already been living and experiencing life for years, the indelible ink of those experiences don't yet begin to permeate upon the canvas of memory. It's as though a child's first few years are written on a chalkboard and placed in an open field, exposed to the elements. Though the child is writing his or her experiences with each day, the words fade over time. Each memory may only last a day or two before the wind or rain comes along and wipes the board clean. I was four and a half when I first traded my chalk for ink and canvas, so to speak, and remember details of the day vividly, as though they occurred only hours ago.

Every morning after recess, the children in my kindergarten class would gather together on the floor for circle time while our teacher, Mrs. Brubaker, read story books. It was my least favorite activity of the day. At least while everyone sat at their desks, I was allowed to immerse myself in workbooks on music theory I brought with me from home. While all the other children travailed to color within the lines and hold their crayons between two pinched fingers, I was studying chords, scales, arpeggios, and the introduction to complex rhythm.

Shortly after my first piano performance at Miss Anne's, my parents purchased a used piano and placed it in the corner of our living room. After it became apparent I was capable of sitting at it for hours at a time each day, it was quickly relocated to my bedroom. Since no one else in the family had musical inclinations, my parents were further persuaded that music tutors would be required. And of course, none of this was in the budget.

I now appreciate much more that the combined salary of a school teacher and a firefighter does not go terribly far. I don't know how my parents did any of it. By the time it became evident my gift would require some investment, I'm sure Mom and Dad were already tapped out. My parents and I owe so much to the kindness of others. Any kind of school for the gifted was not an option, but word spread quickly and soon I found myself surrounded by teachers or friends of my parents willing to help tutor me in music both during school and after. I had three to four tutors at any given time and in those early years, I absorbed it all like a sponge.

Sitting there in the circle with the rest of my kindergarten class, my mind drifted to music and the lessons I would return to later that afternoon. I was already composing in the most rudimentary form and I couldn't wait to experiment with the unique melodic embellishments resonating in my imagination.

All of a sudden, a sound had caught my attention when a breeze outside picked up. The rest of the children remained engrossed in the story as Mrs. Brubaker read on, but there was a tune rising in the distance that caused me to sit up and look for the source. As the wind intensified, so did the volume of the melody. There was something so inviting and familiar in the sound. Without noticing, I was suddenly standing on my feet with my gaze fixed out the window.

"Michael? Michael? Please sit down when I'm reading," Mrs. Brubaker asked politely, while looking up from her book.

But I couldn't hear her. Déjà vu was a concept I had not yet learned, but as the trees swayed in the wind and the tune acquired a clarity in sound, it felt as though I had seen this all somewhere before. Though the language was indecipherable the tune carried a deeply intrinsic meaning to me as though the very genetic code of my DNA became the sheet music from which this choral melody originated. This was my song and — it was becoming clear to me as I stared beyond the windows — the trees were the choir. As the reality of what I was perceiving set in, I burst out of the classroom before Mrs. Brubaker could even raise her voice after me.

I ran as fast as my little legs could carry me towards the forest which lay just beyond the playground and the soccer field. My lungs were burning, and running against the wind made me feel like I was a rocket on rails. I wasn't even five, so catching up to me in the middle of the soccer field probably didn't strain Mrs. Brubaker tremendously. When she grabbed my arm from behind, it startled me and I yelled. We collapsed together in the middle of the field and I could hear her shouting.

"Michael! Michael! What are you doing? Where do you think you're going? You can't just leave the class like that!" Mrs. Brubaker spoke firmly, but even at that age, I knew it came from sincere concern for my wellbeing.

All I could shout in reply was, "Can't you hear them? The trees are singing. The trees are singing!"

"Michael. We're in the middle of circle time. You can't just run out of the class like that!" She said, dismissing my eccentric comments as we both rose from the ground. The grass had stained our knees from the tumble. I could tell Mrs. Brubaker was annoyed. This kind of behavior was out of character for me to say the least. I was often overlooked for being the quiet one and generally remained disengaged from our classroom activities. But that day I heard music and it was coming from the trees.

As my teacher and I returned together through the playground towards our classroom, I could see the faces of all my classmates pressed up against the window, staring in curious wonder at the spectacle I had become. Mrs. Brubaker's hand remained firmly clasped around my wrist as I continued to protest through broken sobs that hurt my still burning lungs. "But the trees were singing! The trees were singing!" It was not the last time I heard their song.

A few years later I was seven years old and in grade one. It was recess and all the other kids played outside while I remained in the classroom alone. I stood in front of the whiteboard with a marker in my hand. Above my head the words *Trees do not sing* had been written by my teacher. Below the words, five empty lines had been drawn – waiting expectantly to be filled in with the same phrase. Five times before recess was over. Those were my instructions.

Though I don't now recall yelling out in the middle of spelling, "The trees! Do you hear that? They're singing again! They're singing!" I do remember standing there staring at those five lines. My teacher—I forget his name—wrote out *Trees do not sing* and then drew the lines, while prattling a quick reprimand before leaving the room as the kids filed out for recess. I don't think he was expecting to see what would evolve in the short time he was gone. In an impulsive flash of inspiration, the five lines before me transposed into empty musical bars. I began to compose.

I quickly discovered that I would need more room as my notes began to fill the spaces in between the lines. Picking up a ruler, I extended them on the board until they touched our classroom weather box, where earlier that morning one of the students had drawn a passable picture of the sun in yellow below the words *Today the weather is*:

I continued to compose. My adrenaline began to surge as I began to write with greater urgency. Not because I knew my time was limited, but because as I wrote out the song I heard coming from the trees for the first time, the music connected to a place deep within my being and once again I was overcome with a profound sense that I had heard it all before. I became compelled to write the song out more than ever as the conviction that this was somehow *my* song grew with every note that appeared on the board. My fingers turned red where I held the marker from pressing so hard on the whiteboard. My entire body was tense, captive to the melody blaring in my heart which no one else could hear.

I had just begun to erase the weather box to make room for more lines when my teacher came back into the classroom. Without saying much, but feeling a deep agitation, he picked up the whiteboard eraser and began to wipe the board clean. To this day I'm still surprised I didn't rile in protest knowing what a precious thing this music was. But I remained calm as the board returned to stark white because I could still hear the music. It was in me. Every note and intonation had been inscribed on the canvas of my mind never to be erased again.

A week later, the notes were re-written with ink and took up seventeen pieces of paper. Today, those pages are behind glass and on display in the east hallway of the Lincoln Center where the New York Philharmonic performs under my direction.

As the youngest musical director the Philharmonic has ever known, I walk the corridor daily on the way to my office, still admiring it every time I pass the piece I composed so long ago. Above it reads, "*Chant Des Arbes*" Symphony in B minor. It was the first full symphony piece I wrote and it became popular only a few years later, before I even turned twelve years old. Since those moments which formed my early memories, I've written 134 other symphonies or musical works and they are known and played by orchestras around the world. But "The Song of The Trees" will always be cherished because it was my first.

Chapter 2: I Will Never Leave You

There's one more memory which has somehow endured in my mind as vividly as the day I experienced it. Ask me anything that may have happened before or after the moment, and I could not tell you. Ask me to try and forget it and I could not. You may as well ask me to try and rise from the dead. On Sundays, we went to church as a family. The Sundays when Dad could join us were everyone's favorite. We would get up early and have a big breakfast together, go to church and afterwards, spend our afternoons at a park or beach. But those Sundays were rare. On most Sundays, breakfast was rushed because all of us kids chose to sleep in since T.V. was not allowed on Sunday mornings. Then Mom would take my sisters and me to church while Dad worked or recovered from a shift at the Fire Hall. This was one of those Sundays.

After a hurried breakfast of cold cereal, I managed to get dressed in my nice shirt and comb my hair to the side with a wet brush. It still stood up in the back, but no one seemed to mind that much, especially me. I was only five and mom was just grateful for my early inclination towards independence.

On the short drive across town, one of my older sisters got to sit up front with Mom while the rest of us sat spread out across the back seats of the van. I was the only one who still needed a booster. As I stared out the window watching our sleepy town pass by, most often in those moments, my thoughts would have been occupied with music—but not this morning.

I had been taught about Jesus and God early in life. I knew

about the cross where Jesus died and I knew about the story of the empty tomb where the big stone had been rolled away. It was all connected to the love God had for the world, and for me. But at the age of five, I could no more understand the vast expanse of that love than I could comprehend the reach of outer space.

But that morning my mind was focused on a prayer I had learned. It was a petition, a commitment, and an invitation. It was simple, yet profound. With this little prayer, I was told that God would come and occupy a place in my heart like a melody occupies a song. Although I had learned about it weeks ago, I had not yet ventured to recite the words. Even then, though I did not fully understand it, I knew the prayer was significant and would change my life forever.

As our van turned at the final intersection along our route and the church came into view, I sensed an acceleration in my heart and felt its pulse intensify against the walls of my chest. Something inside of me in that moment told me it was time. Whether it was unction or simply the desire to not step across the church threshold again without having invited God in, I could not tell. The words just came out:

"Dear Jesus, please come into my heart. Amen."

Unfortunately, it can sometimes be difficult for a five-year-old to gauge the volume of a whisper. My moment of private conversion was overheard by my Mom who quickly voiced her delight with the enthusiasm typical of any proud mother.

"Michael, that's so wonderful! I'm so proud of you. This is a very happy day!" Mom gushed from the driver seat as she turned the corner into the church parking lot.

My five-year-old dignity was bruised, and I could feel my face blush with embarrassment over the boisterous public broadcast calling attention to my private communion with God. Panic set in and without a second thought, I heard myself sputtering the words:

"Go back! Go back!" While frantically flapping my hands in front of my chest as though trying to hold back the encroaching tide on a beach.

That's when I heard another voice.

To this day I could not tell you if it was audible or whispered from within the hallways of my heart—it was that clear. But I can tell you what I heard.

"No." The voice said resoundingly. "I will never leave you and I will never forsake you."

The words resonated in my little heart as heaven's response to my protest settled on me like the first snow of winter, galvanizing the moment forever in my memory. That was the moment I realized the words I recited were more than just a Sunday School tradition. That was the moment I learned that God was real.

Chapter 3: Broken to Pieces

I always assumed my childhood was normal. But of course, to every child still living theirs out, there is no way for them to know much else. Despite my obvious gift, my parents tried their best to keep me surrounded by as much 'normal' as possible. Looking back, I'm sure their own limitations played as much a factor in this as did their best intentions. I had three other siblings and none of them could play the piano at a Level Seven proficiency by the age of six.

My older twin sisters were two individuals who looked practically identical, but could not have been more opposite in their disposition and tastes. Faith had a calculated mind, loved anything glamourous and fashionable and stayed with ballet right up until her senior year of high school. Felicity switched over to Karate during fourth grade, played sports with the boys through school and navigated life wearing her heart on her sleeve. And then there is Madeline. She always had more energy to spare than most. I think Mom and Dad put her in gymnastics at an early age, more in the hopes that it would make her tired at night. By the time I came, it seemed that I was just a tag-a-long with a wide exposure to 'normal childhood' where I was expected to fall in with the rest. I don't think they were expecting the gift I brought into the mix.

By the age of six, I had expanded my repertoire to include the violin and clarinet and had composed my own various concert pieces. I coasted along thinking all of this was just normal as well. But I realize now that I merely observed normal while never really falling into its rhythm. Music was my only momentum in life and I had no desire to fit in with those who were not moved by it.

I wish I could say the same about pain — that I only observed it in others at a distance while I remained impervious to its influence. But I suppose it was the common human condition of pain that made me more 'normal' after all.

My first violin was a used Yamaha my parents bought at a music store. It lacked the sophisticated tone and depth that I could already pick out from a violin solo in a performance, but when fitted with fresh strings, it could produce a cordial sound. While my peers became familiar with the Saturday morning cartoon lineup, I would memorize another concerto by Tchaikovsky or Beethoven and allow the beautiful refrain from my violin strings to stimulate my imagination and whisk me away to famous concert halls around the world where I dreamt I might one day perform.

For my ninth birthday, my parents took me to the Seattle Symphony where the orchestra was playing a tribute to Brahms that evening. I could not hold back my excitement. The forty-five minute drive into Seattle seemed to take hours, as we could not get there soon enough. The anticipation had built over the days leading up to this trip so much that I was no longer permitted to pepper my parents with a fusillade of facts from my knowledge about the orchestra and its members.

Walking into the concert hall was a spiritual experience. As we stepped through the main doors that lead into the vaulted expanse of the auditorium, time slowed to a stop and so did I. Like a monk dawning the entrance of a great cathedral for the first time after a pilgrimage from a distant land, a reverence settled upon me when I stood inside. I could feel the acoustics and was aware of the slightest plink from a string reverberating from the front. In this place, music was free to soar like an eagle released from captivity into the limitless expanse of the sky. The concert had not yet begun but I had already started to feel emotion swell in anticipation of the moment to come.

The concert itself was like floating in isolated hot spring waters with cascading cliff walls on every side to echo back every drop and stir from the pool, with no one else around. I sat at the edge of my chair for the whole performance, not wanting to miss a single detail. I had memorized most of the pieces being played and it took everything within me to not stand up and start conducting in perfect unison with the conductor at the podium.

When the concert was over and the audience started to make their way back towards the lobby my parents remained in their seats. A mischievous grin subtly crept across their faces. I waited until we were practically the only ones remaining in the auditorium when I finally spoke up.

"Mom, aren't we going to go out? Everyone else is leaving."

By now my mom's smile was like contagious laughter that can get a room full of people howling for no reason. She looked at my dad who had the same stupid grin on his face.

"Not yet, honey. Your dad and I have a surprise for you. Just wait and see."

With that, I was gripped with intrigue and I knew something else awaited me that evening. I leaned back in my chair and said nothing while my mind started to race with possibilities. Looking back, it's clear I didn't have a very good imagination because I didn't come close to guessing the incredible gift my parents had premeditated. Ushers came and did a quick sweep of the isles and checked for anyone remaining. One of them made eye contact with my dad and gave him a wink as he passed by. They closed the auditorium doors and it was silent inside. Approaching footsteps on

27

the stage broke the silence as the conductor and his first violinist walked back to the center of it.

"Mann Family? Matthew and Helen?" The conductor called out.

"Hi," my mom said with a goofy wave.

"Would you like to come up and join us on the stage?" The maestro asked with his baton hand outstretched to the side stairs leading up to the stage.

Without hesitation my parents stood and started walking down the aisle towards the front. "Come on, Michael," mom said to me, stopping momentarily to look back. I remained in my seat, feeling immobilized by the initial shock hitting me in the gut. What was happening? It felt like I remained fixed to my chair while time froze and my heart danced wilder than a conductor's baton in an Accelerando. But without noticing I had moved, I found myself at my parents side as we approached the center of the stage.

The conductor stared down at me with a warm smile. "And you, young master, must be Michael?" he said.

I nodded. Words evaporated within me as though I might never speak them again.

The conductor continued. "I've heard so many good things about you. And how old are you young man?"

I heard myself respond: "Nine."

"Michael, I'd like to introduce you to a very good friend of mine, Victor Castellani. He and I have been playing music together now for over twenty-eight years. Can you imagine?" He said with a light-hearted chuckle.

I knew who Victor was. I had listened to his solo records and spent countless hours studying his form as he played in various concert venues. He was famous. And now I was standing on the stage with him while he shook my parents' hands, his violin held loosely in the other. He approached me next and leaned down to speak with me at eye level.

"Hello master Michael," he said. His subtle Italian accent complimented his noble demeanor perfectly. His white hair curled in the back, in contrast with the black tuxedo he wore, which was the only piece of dress I had ever seen him wear.

"Hello," I said. I really liked the sound of 'Master Michael' spoken in an Italian accent. I wish I could have recorded that moment.

"Maestro and I have heard a lot about you and we were wondering, would it be possible for us to hear you play a little something?" As he said this his eyes moved to the violin which he now raised in both hands towards me. As the beautiful instrument shifted in his hands I could see the engraved letters on the back: *D.Z. Strad*. He may as well have been handing me the gift of immortality. This instrument was the apogee of violins, handcrafted with aged spruce and tonewoods from the Italian Alps. Now suspended in his hands only inches from me, I saw the stunned look on my face reflecting back in the sheen of its glassy oil varnish.

Reluctantly and delicately, I lifted the violin and bow from his hands. The conductor brought me a chair as the grownups all sat around close by. The moments that proceeded it were like an out-of-body experience. I could see myself close my eyes as I nestled the instrument below my chin. All the nerves and emotion that had pulsed through me the entire evening were sucked from the room the moment the bow connected to the magnificent instrument making the first stroke. The auditorium filled with a majestic sound that made the angels of heaven pause as though God himself commanded a moment of silence so he could lean in and listen. I was born for this moment.

The tears streaming down my mother's cheeks said it all while the refrain from my last note faded back into silence. And then a single and slow clap... clap... clap from Victor which escalated into a frenzied standing ovation from my audience of four.

Victor approached me once again and settled on one knee in front of where I sat. "That was beautiful. You truly are a master."

The nerves returned where they left off and I found myself grasping for words once again. "Thank you," I managed to offer sheepishly.

Then a familiar and mischievous grin appeared across his face as he spoke again, "What do you think of my violin? Nice isn't it?"

"Oh, it's amazing," was the most generous reply I could find.

"Well, master Michael, it is yours. Happy birthday to you, my boy."

My mom's checked emotions could no longer remain held back as she burst into sobbing laughter. I looked into her tear-stained eyes and my face said the words I could not give a voice to: *Is this really happening?*

She nodded her head as she tried the best she could to wipe her face with a saturated and mangled Kleenex crumpled in her hand. My dad held one arm around her shoulder as my eyes went from hers to his only to find that they were moist as well.

The rest of the evening seemed to fade from my memory. I don't remember the conversation after or the drive home. And I wonder, thinking back to the moment when we would have had to say our goodbyes and walk out of the auditorium, if my feet even touched the ground.

I cherished my new violin for three wonderful months. I would have worn velvet gloves while playing if I knew it wouldn't have muffled the sound.

I should never have taken it with me to school.

After months of trying to persuade me to join the rest of the kids who played outside during recess, my teachers finally relented to my requests and allowed me to remain inside the classroom to read or practice an instrument. Even though I still had my original Yamaha violin, I could not bring myself to return to its sound after growing accustomed to the full-bodied vibrancy of my precious D.Z. Strad. Could a parent ever find as much fulfillment in holding a doll after knowing the warmth of their newborn child?

I was immersed in a violin solo alone in the room when Travis Bishop came and stood in the classroom doorway. Though, supposedly he was a nine-year-old boy like myself, he seemed to fill the entire frame with his imposing figure like an eclipse of the sun. He had a bruise under his left eye which added to his threatening occupation of the doorway – my only path of escape. A tremor of fear pulsed through my tense body like someone who has stumbled across the path of a charging bull elephant.

Travis had only been in our school for a month. He appeared on our class list halfway through the year. He was a military kid and his father was a Marine who was transferred to bases around the country on a moment's notice. Ours was the second school he had attended that year. After only a week in class, his reputation as a rough and mean kid had been established. In gym, he threw a dodgeball at Samuel Johnson's face and gave him a nosebleed. Travis laughed while Samuel crumbled in pain, spattering the gym floor with crimson drops. Travis feigned an apology when confronted by the teacher but after school, he tracked Samuel down in the playground and said, "Hey kid, don't you ever get me in trouble again." Then he kicked Sam in the genitals, doubling him over for the second time that day. I don't know if Samuel or anyone in the playground who witnessed the exchange ever told a teacher about it out of fear of further retribution.

"Hey, let me try that," Travis said as he began to close in on me in the corner of the room where I sat. The hairs on the back of my neck stood like the rigid points on a rake and the adrenaline of flight surged through my body which was still stuck frozen to my chair. Before I knew it he was right over top of me and I caught a sharp waft of pungent pubescent body odor. Before I could yell or say anything he grabbed my violin out of my hands.

"No! You can't have that!" I screamed as I catapulted out of my chair after my prized possession.

With one hand Travis pushed me, causing me to fall backwards over my chair. My head hit the ground hard when I landed. Travis started to play my violin producing a piercing sound that curdled my blood and rang in my ears. I remember laying on the floor listening to the awful shrill and feeling the surge of anger build like dark and heavy clouds ready to let loose their thunder. Rage quickly overpowered the fear I had felt only moments ago. Before I knew it the words were out of my mouth like a cannon blast across the bow of an enemy ship.

"You're just a stupid dumb loser who's too stupid to know that nobody likes you!"

The shrill cacaphony from my violin stopped and time was imprisoned in a cold cage of ominous premonition. Our eyes met with a flash of pure hatred like two live wires connecting in a burst of pyrotechnics. I saw the subtle raise in his eyebrow and knew evil had whispered its intent into his ear. I felt helpless, like being

32

trapped in a nightmare you can't wake out of, and watched as Travis raised my violin above his head and brought it down against our classroom wall with a force that shattered it into pieces. The sound it made as the wood splintered was harrowing. It was the sound of my soul being crushed.

My scream was so turbulent I don't know how the windows in the room did not shatter. The cry was loud enough to attract my teacher who ran into the room and quickly assessed the scene. I remained crumpled and bawling on the floor beside the toppled chair while Travis held the fractured remains of my violin in his hand. Had I paid Travis any attention in that moment, I would have noticed his demeanor change and the color drain from his face. But I had been reduced to a shattered mass on the floor along with the pieces of my violin.

"Travis! What did you do? You come with me right now!" The remains of my violin fell from Travis's hand and hit the floor; my ruin was complete. I don't know how long I stayed on the floor, but it seemed as though hours passed while I hemorrhaged tears until the carpet pressing against my face was saturated. I was inconsolable and refused to move while teachers attempted to offer any comfort they could. My entire class had to stay outside in the playground well after the bell announced the end of recess until my mother could come from the high school and take me home.

I didn't return to school for the rest of that week. I don't even remember if I ate. I was paralyzed, numb, and mute while the aftershocks of the incident ran their course. The only thing that began to offer any comfort were my manufactured mental images of what I would do to Travis Bishop if I ever saw him again.

I never saw Travis back at school after the incident. He was gone. I didn't know what happened to him. I didn't care. Life would carry on but I would never be the same. A subtle shift crept into my life, the way a key change to a minor in a song invokes a sense of foreboding. All I had ever known until that time was love in its simplest and purest form, for my music and my family. But the lens of innocence through which I perceived life became shaded. I knew what it was to hate.

***

My encounter with the conductor at the Seattle Symphony would turn out to be more than an isolated event. I received an invitation from the symphony to play with them later that year and my career took off. One performance led to more invitations in larger venues and before long I was playing in symphony orchestras all over the country. I was quickly emerging as a news phenomenon in the music world. Eventually, I received another D.Z. Strad, but it could never replace the significance of the one from my birthday which had been handed down to me from the hands of a master. It was gone forever, and so was my childhood.

***

My dad couldn't tell the difference between a treble clef and a trombone and you certainly didn't want him to sing for you, under any circumstance. But he was still my hero. Once my travels started to take me across the country and beyond, my dad often couldn't accompany me on the longer trips because of his work. Although he was a committed father, he was also a committed firefighter. It was evident to us he loved what he did and loved the people he worked with, even though some days the strain and fatigue would wear through his strong exterior after a long succession of shifts or attending a heartbreaking scene.

But whether he was Platoon Captain Matthew Mann or just Dad, he could always be counted on to lend his gentle strength and quiet confidence in any situation for all who depended on him.

My dad was a man of few words and yet at moments throughout my childhood he seemed to know just what I needed to hear. One memory stands out more than most. I stood in the hallway of my house, a six-year-old boy in pajamas and a Superman housecoat. My dad was in the kitchen getting ready for his shift, pouring a cup of coffee. The sun had not yet begun to penetrate the cracks in our window blinds.

"Hey buddy. What are you doing up so early? It's not time to wake-up yet," my dad said as he looked up.

"Hi Daddy," I said. I walked right up to him and wrapped my arms around his leg. As he put his hand on my head I started to cry.

"Oh, what's wrong bud?" In a moment he was on his knees eye to eye with me, his strong calloused hands resting on my shoulder.

"You're not mad at me are you?" I asked in childlike quandary.

"Of course I'm not mad at you. Why would I be mad?" By this time he had me in a full embrace while I continued to sniffle quietly on his shoulder.

"I thought you might want me to be a firefighter like you one day, but I don't want to be a firefighter."

"Oh son. Son. You don't have to be a firefighter. Do you know how proud I am of you?" Expecting him to say something about my musical gift, I was caught off guard by what came next. "When you were born and I held you for the first time in my arms do you know what I said to you?"

"No."

"I said, 'Son. I am so proud of you and I'll never stop loving you no matter what.'"

"You said that?"

"Yes, I did. And do you think you were able to do anything more than just poop, cry, and sleep when you were just a little baby?"

"No."

"That's right. I didn't know how amazing you would be with music or that you would have such a kind heart. But I've been proud of you before you could even say a word. So Michael, do you think I'm going to be proud of you no matter what you do?"

"Yes," I answered.

"You bet I am." The sniffles had subsided, but he was still eye to eye with me, with his hand on my shoulder. The conversation was finding its resolve, but there was one more thing.

"Daddy, do you have to go to work? I don't want you to leave."

"Oh buddy, I'll be right back before you know it. I'm not going anywhere."

Chapter 4: The Fire

The call came through at 9:26 a.m. on a Wednesday morning in July. Captain Matthew Mann had just finished having breakfast with his platoon at Marysville Fire District, Station 61, and was finishing kitchen clean up when the tone interrupted their routine. "Apartment structure fire. Fourth floor. 8877 Sixty-fifth Street N.E. Be advised, child, age nine, confirmed trapped inside... All units..." No one heard anything else after that as a surge of adrenaline pulsed through the station sending men racing for their gear and waiting trucks. Rescue truck 221 screamed out of the hall followed by pumper seventeen and ladder forty-nine seconds apart in a frenzied display of light and sound.

Matt rode in the passenger seat playing in his mind the first few steps that he would take and the equipment he would grab the second the truck came to a stop. The column of black smoke appeared in the distance as the truck turned at an intersection, screaming through a red light. The smoke appeared as the only cloud in an otherwise clear sky and cast a shadow as it dissipated in the atmosphere, blocking the sun and darkening the day.

"Step on it, Pete!" Matt yelled.

In most minor incidents, as the captain, Matt would stand back and provide oversight and coordination at the scene. His entire platoon had trained and fought fires together for years. which had galvanized a culture of respect and mutual trust. Every man and woman knew their job and they did it with excellence and efficiency. In that sense, this fire would be no different and he knew his team would not hesitate to go above the call. But one thing was certain in Matt's mind, if anyone was going to be stepping into danger first, it would be him.

The truck pulled up to the apartment and before the wheels came to a stop, a middle-aged woman was pounding on the side of the firetruck door, her eyes wild with panic and desperation.

"My boy! You've got to save my boy! He's in there. Please! Save him!"

Neighbors rushed in to grab the mother and clear her from the firetruck doors and she crumpled on their shoulders in a convulsing and broken wail. Matt stepped off the truck and though he looked calm on the outside, his fear matched the fury of the fire he could see raging from the top floor of the apartment building. By this point it was already out of control. "Peter, you've got control on scene. Don't hit it direct until you've got word from us that we've got the boy. Jones, Meyers, Lewis, you're up the stairs with me." Matt grabbed rescue rope and an axe and began to run towards the building. He didn't have to turn back to know the others were right there with him.

Just as he entered the door he heard the mother screaming again, "Dear Jesus save my boy! Save my boy!"

As he took the stairs in 2 steps at a time, Matt was praying the same thing. "Jesus, let me find the boy alive."

The smoke got thick on the third floor. Peter came in through Matt's radio as he and the team stepped into the fourth floor hallway. "Captain, the flames have broken through the roof. Structure overhead is going to be compromised. This is out of control. Get out of there as quick as you can. How copy?"

"Copy Peter. We're on it."

"Oh, and Captian, the boy's name is Thomas. Be careful up there."

"Ten. Four."

The radiant heat from the fire burning in the roof cavity could be felt in the hallway on the fourth floor as the team now carefully approached its source. Without their oxygen tanks it would have been impossible to breathe. The acrid smoke limited their visibility to the man standing beside them and nothing beyond. Debris was already to starting to fall from the ceiling as they stood outside of apartment number 419. They didn't need to check the door for heat. It was all around them. Matt kicked in the door and jumped back as a wall of flame erupted into the hallway with the fury of hell. "Captain, we can't go in there!" Lewis yelled over the roar. But before Lewis could even finish, Matt jumped across the threshold of apartment 419.

Every moment was measured by seconds. Had Matt hesitated only a few more after kicking in the door, his only entry into the apartment would have been barricaded by a falling maelstrom of joists and beams that were now nothing more than savage embers. Matt was trapped inside, separated from the rest of his crew. Unable to hear them calling his name through the roar of the blaze licking up the walls and ceiling around him, he began crawling forward towards what appeared to be a bedroom calling out, "Thomas! Thomas!"

The smoke inside made it impossible to see. It was hailing hot embers and debris. Matt could hear the building straining to hold itself up with its deteriorating members groaning and cracking all around him. Just as he crawled through a doorway his hand bumped against the form of a body. "Thomas!" Matt quickly took off his glove and felt for breathing—nothing. A pulse—faint. "It's okay, buddy. My name is Captain Matthew Mann and I'm going to get you out of here. Just hang on." It was impossible for Matt to remove his mask or perform any kind of resuscitation. Oxygen had been sucked from the space. The boy's only chance at life was to get him out of the building and onto the ground—and fast. Matt took the rescue rope from around his shoulders and began to secure one end around Thomas. Thin fingers of faint light were seen reaching through the thick smoke which told Matt that a window was nearby.

From his place on the ground where Peter had control of the scene, he could tell that his crews had no control of the fire. Another window above blew out followed by more black smoke like discharge from a bellowing culvert. "Lieutenant! Look!" There was a second's pause in the flurry of activity below as everyone stopped to see the body of nine-year-old Thomas being hoisted out of the window and slowly lowered down by a lifeline. No one had to shout an instruction before there were eight firefighters and two paramedics running to the base of the building directly below where Thomas was being lowered. Thomas landed in the outstretched arms of safety and was carried out of harm's way towards a waiting ambulance.

Matt came to the window to see his patient being worked on outside the ambulance below. "Thank you, Jesus," he said out loud. To his relief, he could also see his three crew members who followed him up, safely back on the ground below. He gave them all a thumbs up from the window while they turned their focus to extricating their captain and extinguishing the fire. The pumper trucks were in position and the ladder truck was slowly reaching for the fourth floor window like the outstretched arms of an angel.

For the first time since he stepped foot on the scene, he could feel the tension in his body. Only moments ago, his only single concern had been for the safety and lives of others. Sensations he had been numb to now woke up within him. He could feel the weight of his oxygen tank pulling down on his shoulders. The excessive heat all around him transformed his turnout gear into an oven and the fog inside his mask from his heavy breathing was the only remnant of moisture that remained within the fury of the hungry inferno.

The ladder truck had almost reached their captain when a low groan signaled the start of the collapse. The exterior walls and columns around where the fire burned the hottest gave out under the strain from the failing structure above. The crash caused flames to leap up in a fury like a pack of wild beasts taking down their prey. The army of first responders below could only watch in horror as their captain was swallowed by the hungry holocaust of debris and blaze.

***

I was practicing scales in my room when I heard my mother scream. I ran into the hallway towards the direction of the sound. My sisters came running from the living room and met me in the hallway. We continued together in a mad dash as a mob. Stopping ten feet short of our front door, we all stood like sculptures and took in the unusual scene before us. My mother had fallen into the arms of the fire chief and Lieutenant Peter Oakley who both stood side by side in our entrance. Behind them I could see two firetrucks parked out front of our house with their lights on. Firefighters were congregated outside on our lawn, their helmets dawned and tucked under their arms. All of them had taken a knee. The chief stood with a wide-eyed stare of somber disbelief as he wrapped his arms around my mother while she wept. Peter was wearing full fire gear. His face was covered in black soot except where his tears cut a line down the sides of his face exposing pink skin as they rolled down in a steady stream. He looked up with red somber eyes and extended his arm out to us. "Come here kids. Come here." His voice cracked as he spoke. In his hand he held a familiar firefighter's helmet covered in abrasions and soot. Below the crest of the Marysville Fire Department on the helmet it read Cpt. Mann.

I was twelve years old.

Chapter 5: The Funeral

Every flag in Washington State and across the country flew at half-mast. My dad's heroic rescue had made international headlines and fire halls all over were standing with their brothers and sisters in Marysville. He was America's hero and today they were laying him to rest. An elegant white limousine pulled up in front of our house. Two columns of police motorcycles along with police cars and fire trucks formed an escort at the front while two more fire trucks and police cars followed up the rear. If it had been for any other occasion, I would have looked on our entourage in wonder. But today I just felt like staring at the ground. Everyone along the entire block of our neighborhood stood outside by their front doors. Some of the kids I rode bikes with were holding small American flags while their parents stood behind them and wept.

Peter Oakley and his wife rode with us in the limousine. My dad and Peter had become close friends over the years and us kids had adopted them as Auntie and Uncle Oakley, which I think suited them just fine. They had no kids of their own, but still came over often for dinners and barbeques. They sat one on each side of my mother with Madeline curled up in a ball on Mom's lap. Madeline and my other two sisters had no problem showing their emotion. The limo was filled with the sound of their quiet intermittent sobs for the whole hour up to Seattle where dad's memorial service was being held. I sat on an end seat where I could stare out the window.

The streets of Marysville were packed shoulder to shoulder with locals and pilgrims alike come to pay their respects. Each one stared at our limo as it went by, their tear-stained eyes trying to get a glimpse of the family inside. Thank God for tinted windows.

Our entourage grew to 137 fire trucks, police cars, and various E.M.S. vehicles that stretched over a mile long before we left Marysville and merged onto the I-5. I could hear the subdued pulse of news helicopters above which followed us most of the way. I fought the lumpy swell of emotion back as it began to look for an exit at the sight of mourners along our way. At every overpass, first responders stood shoulder to shoulder along the side rail in full dress or turnouts and held a salute. Often, set up right behind them, was an American flag suspended between two raised truck ladders.

At one overpass they had draped a banner over the side which read, "God Bless Cpt. Matthew Mann." At that, a silent tear was finally able to break away and crest down my cheek. I wiped at it savagely with my sleeve as a surge of anger enveloped me displacing any sorrow I had allowed myself to feel in that moment. I could no more rage against the fire that took my dad's life than I could at a mythological beast. But I could rage at the One who did nothing to save him. God didn't bless my dad. He killed him.

Memorial Stadium in downtown Seattle was full to capacity with additional hundreds seated on chairs set up in the playing field surrounding the podium set up in the center. Another crowd was gathered outside the stadium congregating around speakers and a large screen. Flowers were stacking up at makeshift memorials back in Marysville, at the scene of the fire and outside the stadium doors. The funeral was being carried across national and state T.V. outlets across the country, giving the world their opportunity to feast on the drama of our family's tragedy like a pack of feral dogs gorging themselves on a carcass.

While everyone converged around our family like a crushing

swell, I was retreating deep into the caverns of my mind, burning the bridges to my heart as I went. There was nothing to be gained from community or emotion. They could not bring my dad back any more than a dance could bring the rain. Besides, no one felt the loss as deeply as me. There was no one who understood my pain. I never felt so alone.

Nine-year-old Thomas Hudson sat among the dignitaries with his mother and the rest of the Hudson family a few rows back from the front where I sat. The first responders who received him on the other end of my dad's life line that day were able to bring him back quickly and only sent him to hospital for observation. News crews were practically kicking down the hospital doors to get the full story once they learned the apartment fire involved a firefighter's heroic rescue and his subsequent line of duty death. The faces of Thomas Hudson and his mom Nancy, started to appear in headlines and news reports along with my father's service picture and scenes from the fire.

Nancy Hudson was a single mother, aged thirty-four, who worked two part-time jobs while taking care of her three children. Thomas was the only one home when the fire broke out and must not have heard the smoke alarms over the noise of his video game blaring in his headphones. His mom was at work and his sisters were out with friends. Though the cause of the fire was still under investigation, initial reports suggested that a stove element was accidently left on when Nancy left the house causing a nearby dish cloth to catch fire. In every interview that Nancy was in, she was holding Thomas in a crushing embrace while she bellowed out thanks to God and to that firefighter who saved her boy. I only saw the interview once and it was enough. How I wished it had been Thomas and not my dad.

The din of bagpipes broke through the silence of the anticipating mourners as the procession of the honor guard made its way onto the field of Memorial Stadium. The crowd stood to their feet as row after row of decorated first responders filed in behind the pipes and the drums. It was evident from the solemn tear-stained faces that most of them had embraced the grieving process well before their turn to march in. The crowd roiled as another wave of grief hit them like a baton passed in a race.

My mom stood tall and proud with her arms around my sisters while they clung to her and sobbed. She carried the weight of her own sorrow with a brave face; an empty stare gazing into a future where memories were all she could hold of her husband. I knew she was trying to be strong for us. But as the honor guard passed by, the tears glistening on her cheeks betrayed the torrent of emotion trapped inside.

I kept my mind focused on the music from the procession itself. One piper was playing slightly sharp which isn't hard to do and a snare drum in the second row needed tightening.

The refrain from the dirge called to a sorrow residing deep inside which I chose to disavow like a defeated foe banished beyond an impassable ocean. My mind fought to stay fixed on the ligature of melodies and notes which could be measured and understood—where my pain was something that could not. As I visualized more notes finding their rightful place within the lines of the staff and the rules of rhythm, my distain for those who could mourn around me grew. The truth was, I longed to access the liberating release that came with tears, but chose to feed my anger and let my heart starve.

The music finally subsided and the speeches began. Among those who spoke were the mayor and fire chief of Marysville. Peter

Oakley followed with a word on behalf of the family. Peter read from prepared notes while he fought to maintain his composure. His speech was a tapestry of humorous moments provoking the crowd to laughter, woven between touching memories of Matthew Mann: a father, husband, friend, and hero. As Peter resumed his seat, I saw him bury his face in his hands as a fresh wave of sorrow overtook him causing his whole body to quiver.

Another man dressed in a decorated firefighter's uniform came to the podium. "Seattle Fire Chief Theodore Perry will now read the Firefighter's Prayer," came an announcement from the front. Standing erect and dignified behind the podium, the chief began.

"It is now my honor to read to you the Firefighter's Prayer," he said.

"When I am called to duty, God, wherever flames may rage,
Give me strength to save a life, whatever be its age.

Let me embrace a little child before it is too late,
or save an older person from the horror of that fate.

Enable me to be alert to hear the weakest shout,
and quickly and efficiently to put the fire out.

I want to fill my calling to give the best in me,
To guard my friend and neighbor and protect their property.

And if according to Your will, while on duty I must answer death's call;
bless with Your protecting hand my family, one and all."

The Firefighter's Prayer, by AW Smokey Linn.

The chief maintained his composure for the reading, until he came to the last lines. As his voice cracked and waned with the final words of the poem, there was another shift in the semblance of the crowd and grief spilled into the stadium like the surge of an artesian well. There was no immediate movement from the chief when the reading ended, as if to acknowledge the reverence of the moment. The crowd took their time to catch their breath before another man approached the stage.

Our pastor wore no uniform nor did he portray an air of distinction. He was modestly outfitted in jeans and a plain shirt underscored with brown leather shoes and a blue sport blazer. Every Sunday this same man would stand at the front of our church in Marysville and talk to us about the love of God. I could tell by the redness in his eyes that he too had been tossed about in the sea of emotion with the crowd today. But now as he was approaching the microphone, there was a peace that accompanied him as though he were walking across still water.

"My name is Pastor Steve. I'm one of the pastors at the church where Captain Mann attended. I'm here today because his family has asked me to say a few words."

As Pastor Steve entered into his message, he walked out from behind the podium to the edge of the platform and began to pace back and forth along its edge, always facing out and looking up as one trying to engage the audience in an intimate heart to heart. He had their full attention.

"There are a lot of us who really struggle when we have to face a loss like this in life, not just with the emotions and the grief but with God himself. *'God, why did this great man have to die?'* We will either shout this question into the air or whisper it under our breath in muffled sobs. And then, as in most cases like these, we will wait for an answer that doesn't seem to come." He stopped his pacing for a moment and stood still, looking into the crowd. As if to reinforce his statement, the stadium fell profoundly silent.

"And I don't have the answer to this question. But I do have a response. God is there in those moments. He is with us in our grief. And he's not just standing by as an observer." His shoe could be heard dragging on the stage from the back seats of the stadium as he resumed his pacing. As he spoke, his gesturing hands reinforced his articulation.

"He has fully entered into our pain and grief with us. While we rail at heaven with our 'Why God' questions, he stands right alongside with us—weeping and broken hearted by the same hurt that generates the questions we struggle with. You see, God does not create our pain. He walks through it, entering into it with us. It's why he sent His son Jesus to walk the dusty roads of humanity. God with us. And it's why we have the cross. Because not only did God, in His great love for us, take on our pain but our sin that separated us from him as well. God longs so much to be with us, to befriend us in every season of the soul…"

Though the pastor continued to speak, his words drifted off into unintelligible sound as the weight of my own darkness settled upon my shoulders and whispered into my ears.

"God is not your friend."

"He doesn't care about you."

"You're completely alone."

The statements burgeoned in my pain like an invasive species planted in a fragile ecosystem before thriving on its destruction. They were the only words I could hear.

The pastor took his seat as a bell was brought to the platform by two color guard members. Two others followed carrying a side table upon which was placed my dad's service helmet. It had been polished since the day Peter held it in his hands at our front door—the day my life changed forever. The bell was placed beside my

49

dad's helmet at the center of the stage suspended in silence. Waiting.

The fire chief stepped to the microphone and explained the significance of the bell holding our attention on the platform. They sounded it eight times with a methodical cadence breaking the reverent silence with acute peals of sound. Every signal from the bell hit my heart with a concussive blow until it ceased to flow with purpose and vitality leaving behind a listless pulse sustaining the lifeless anatomy of a boy who had died inside. The guns came next.

As my dad's casket was being carried out on the shoulders of the honor guard through straight lines of decorated men in salute, a firing party in the distance released three volleys into the air. The report of the guns ripped through the silence and galvanized my resolve with every round. "God if you're listening, I'll never speak with you again. I hate you."

Chapter 6: The Collapse

The day of Dad's funeral was a long time ago and life, as they say, carried on even though a piece of me remained in the moment they lowered his body in the ground. I remember resenting the fact we had to walk away when the last prayer had been uttered around his grave and yield to the relentless momentum of life like underwater flora caught in the ocean's ceaseless sway. It rained that afternoon as we drove home from the funeral cloaking the last half of the day in a fitting grey. As we drove, I remember my mom telling us all that the sun would shine again. Maybe, I thought, but I wanted it to stand still.

But music still moved me. While a small part of me remained standing by my dad's graveside, the rest of me was carried away by the melodic sounds of symphonies and sonatas. I worked harder than ever, writing new music, accepting every invitation I received to play in concert halls near and far. I was growing up fast, leaving the tattered fragments and memories of my childhood behind.

I grew in my career, craft, and years. The momentum of life had me in its grasp and was thrusting me on an upward trajectory towards celebrity faster and farther than any of my colleagues or counterparts of the day. I moved to New York when I was just eighteen to take up a full-time position playing with the New York Philharmonic. By the young age of twenty-two, I was its musical director, making me the youngest person by decades to ever hold such an illustrious position.

It seemed as though my pace would only continue to quicken

and I was only just beginning my adult life. But a wall was coming. One day, in a single moment, everything would stop.

I remember the day starting out as every other. I left my apartment on Central Park West at seven o' clock and started my walk to work. As was my routine, I would stop at my favorite coffee shop for a tall black coffee and an oven-fired bagel with plain cream cheese. My wife, Jessie, was still asleep in bed when I left and would most likely stay there until nine or nine-thirty. Our housekeeper would arrive at eight-thirty and have breakfast and coffee ready when she awoke. Jessie would not instruct her first yoga class until two o' clock later that afternoon.

We married each other young, when I was only twenty-two and she had just turned twenty. Our honeymoon on the Mexican Riviera held the makings of a dream — drinking in each other's love late into each night and sleeping in each other's arms long into the mornings. After a simple ceremony on the beach, we danced barefoot in the sand to the rhythm of breakers and a mariachi band. I told her I loved her that day and in her eyes saw a girl emerging from the shadows where she had hidden herself away, a vulnerability I swore to myself then I would cherish and protect. There were moments, too, when I found myself venturing beyond the borders of my fortified heart, traversing the edges of an open field where I could be known. But retreat was a reflex I had nurtured for too long and I found myself returning behind walls where feeling could not find me — and like all good dreams, our honeymoon came to an end.

We certainly thought we loved each other at the time, but if we were honest, our motives for coming together had not been altruistic from the start. Ambition and accolades filled a void, driving me deeper into a lifestyle of performance both on and off the stage. I had just become the youngest musical director in the

New York Philharmonic Orchestra with my profile making the cover of *Time Magazine* and *Rolling Stone*, just to name a few. My brand was burgeoning in an accumulation of distinctions and awards and she was one of the most outgoing and gorgeous creatures I had ever encountered—a suitable prize among a collection of others.

Where I was more introverted and demure, Jessie didn't live a moment in that lane. She sought attention from anyone who was willing to give it to her—especially if that someone had money and stature. Her alluring figure was often on display in her skin-tight workout attire—her best attempt at modesty—which is how she first got my attention. When she cast longing eyes on me I could not escape her pull. She was my adrenaline rush and I was her stability and status. We don't all marry for love.

The evening before was typical of how most of our time together had been playing out lately. I arrived home to find dinner ready in the fridge which our housekeeper had prepared that afternoon. I could hear Jessie in our bedroom with the shower on and figured she must have just returned from her last class. I took dinner out of the fridge, placed it on the stove to warm, and began to set the table.

"Oh, you're home already. I thought you'd be working late again tonight," Jess said as she stepped into the kitchen, dressed in her comfortable clothes and still drying her hair with a towel.

"Don't sound so excited to see me," I replied coolly, not looking up from my work.

"Well, let me at least set the table. Hang on a sec. I need to get something." Jessie stepped into the living room and returned with a vase of fresh flowers—an assortment of roses, lilies, and heather. This time I looked up.

"Where did those come from?" I probed with an eyebrow raised.

Jess placed the vase on the center of the table and fussed with them while a smug expression crept across her face. "Oh, just a client who appreciates all I do."

"It must feel nice to be appreciated," I continued acrimoniously, while placing our dinner on the table. Dinner I had paid for. Hell, I had paid for it all, hadn't I? Where was my appreciation? I chafed as I brooded quietly to myself. She didn't reply, but instead brought out her phone and took a picture of the elegant table which she, no doubt, would add to her social media exhibit for the world to admire.

For some reason, her silence generated my need to strike some kind of point as an underlying irritation with her grew. "Jess, it's like you're trying to live in a dollhouse where everything always has to be per..." I would have said 'perfect' to complete my thrust, but was cut off by the flower vase being hurled at my head and had to dodge quickly. The vase smashed against the wall behind me and sent porcelain shrapnel flying in every direction; flowers falling everywhere like limp corpses.

"What the hell, Jess?" I yelled. But my protest could not match the fury erupting from my wife.

"How would you know how I'm trying to live you asshole? You're never around! All you've ever cared about is your stupid music!" She screamed the words at the top of her lungs before bursting into tears, retreating to our room, and slamming the door behind her. No doubt neighbors all around us heard it through the walls and floors. But this was not the first time.

It was hard to predict when her storms of the soul would roll in and ignite in peals of thunder and bolts of fire—even harder to understand where they were coming from. We both had our secrets; I was sure of it. But we were both creatures of the surface, never wanting to venture into each other's depths, afraid of what vile monsters from the past might awaken. Afraid our own might return and devour what little we managed to contrive into our storybook façade.

I came into the room hours later that night, after cleaning up the kitchen which included picking up the carnage from the vase off the floor. Jessie was curled up in a fetal position on her side of the bed, her back towards where I slept as always. An empty wine bottle and glass stained with rose residue and lipstick rested on her bedside table and a pile of crumpled Kleenex lay strewn across the floor below her—another common scene these days. I could tell by her breathing she was still awake. She had her earbuds in and was listening to her music, still waiting for the wine to finally take her.

Part of me wanted to say something but the words were not there. They never were. I undressed and settled quietly into my side of the bed. I placed earbuds of my own in and lay my head on my pillow. We both lay motionless, only inches away, but miles apart as music from our different worlds and scenes from another life played inexorably in our heads until sleep finally and mercifully took us both.

On my walk to the office the next morning, I passed Alfie in his regular spot and dropped a dollar in his guitar case, which held his most valuable worldly possession when he wasn't playing it on the street. If you were to see Alfie's guitar at a garage sale with a sticker that read five dollars, you would probably want to haggle a bit and not pay more than three. How it still even produced a sound was remarkable to me, but there was something so honest and pure about that the music he pulled out of those tired strings which quickly endeared this familiar homeless man to me.

"Well, thank you, Mr. Mann! Bless you. Bless you real good.

Hey, if you're ever wanting to invite me to play in that fancy orchestra of yours, you know it's going to cost you more than that," he said with a friendly wink while he continued to strum.

His words were enriched with an amiable drawl from the South and often lighthearted in nature, conveying a deep sincerity and love for life. Alfie was African American and if I had to guess, I would have placed him in his sixties. Despite his age, he still appeared spry, young and full of vitality every day I saw him. For a man of seemingly no address he kept himself as respectable and clean as one could while being limited to the handouts from a Salvation Army donation bin. He dawned a worn out Yankees ball cap that sat loosely on his head. A brandish of grey could be seen around his sides slowly overtaking the short black hair resembling frost that slowly spreads up the sides of a window on a cold day. He wore an old knitted sweater with patterns and colors that had faded over the years. A thin blue windbreaker kept his sweater dry in a drizzle and his olive green corduroy pants were worn at the knees and frayed at the bottom where they skirted around his old sneakers.

"I know, Alfie. I can't afford you," I said with a smile as I continued to walk on by without slowing my pace.

"You have yourself a wonderful day Mr. Mann! God bless you!" He called out after me.

I bristled at the mention of God, but there was always something that seemed to warm my heart from the exchange we had each morning. I had access to the greatest musical accomplishment in the world, but Alfie's music seemed to possess a depth and essence beyond my reach. *How is that even possible?* I thought.

A few weeks earlier as I walked by Alfie in his regular spot and exchanged the usual banter, a strange scene flashed across my mind—like a vision or daydream. I wouldn't have thought much about it, but after that single occurrence, it started to happen every time I walked by. It was the same scene every time. After a week of this I'd try to intentionally think of something else as I approached Alfie: my music, naked women—anything! Still it would intrude like an unwelcome guest barging through a door I seemed to be powerless to lock.

In the scene, a horse was standing in a large field full of lush green grass. There was shade, fresh water, other horses, anything a horse could ever want, presumably—I know nothing about horses. The field had to be at least a hundred acres or more with a fence all around the perimeter. But this horse in my vision would just stand at the edge of the fence and stare out towards the arid landscape beyond—which seemed really odd. Capturing this horse's attention seemed to be a plain yellow flower sprouting up through parched soil. The fragrant aroma it expelled kept the horse pinned to the side of the fence, while the rest of the herd grazed in the middle of the field. It seemed as though it would have been willing to exchange the entirety of its field for a taste of the single flower. Once again this morning, as I dropped the dollar in Alfie's case, the vision flashed across my imagination. *Do I need to see a psychiatrist one of these days?* I wondered to myself.

I rounded the corner on Sixty-fifth street and stepped into the side entry of the David Geffen Hall in the Lincoln Center—my home away from home. Rehearsal wouldn't start for another six or so hours, but I felt more comfortable in my office than in my apartment. My wife and I led very different lives these days. Generally speaking, our lives seemed happier if we weren't living them together in the same room. Besides, I was continuously composing and the seclusion and privacy of my office offered the

57

best environment for that.

I walked past my "history wall" where my first musical composition, "*Chant Des Arbres*," remained memorialized along with a tapestry of my other numerous accomplishments. When I first began to play with the Philharmonic, I walked this same hall and coveted a place of my own among its canonized works and celebrated composers. I knew if one day I saw my own works enshrined with all the others, I would have finally joined the few elect bright stars in our world — chosen constellations who stood out among a host of billions of others navigating the galaxies in obscurity. But that day as I walked down the hall where my works now outnumbered the rest, I somehow still felt lost, like I was navigating life itself in obscurity.

Yeah. Maybe I better see a psychiatrist.

Over the past month, *Vanity Fair* had been hounding my office for an interview. It was supposed to be more of what they called a 'life piece.' In most interviews, questions about my childhood and background would come up, but they often remained centered around my music leaving all the other less important details off to the side — where I preferred they remain.

With the exception of being a musical prodigy, I had a fairly normal upbringing. Of course I was raised well, surrounded by loving family, and I attended good schools; all around, I had a fairly relatable life with no dark secrets of abuse or neglect hiding in the shadows. It was no secret that my dad died when I was young so we could often address that with one or two questions and move on without the need for deep introspection. So why then, was I so reluctant to bring up the past? What remained hidden in the recesses of my soul that could trigger an unsolicited detonation of anxiety or rage? Maybe I wasn't much different than Jessie after all. For whatever reason, navigating my past was like traversing an abandoned mine field where one wrong step could be harrowing — even fatal.

"So Director... uh, do you mind if I call you Michael?"

Paul Waverley, the columnist for *Vanity Fair* and I sat across from each other in my office. A digital recorder perched attentively on my desk between us taking in every word, absorbing every hesitation and documenting every underlying implication.

"Michael is fine," I replied casually as I leaned back in my chair.

Paul was a short man, making up for what he lacked in stature with eccentric style. From the perspective of the everyday minimalist man, nothing Paul wore made sense or matched. His slacks were woven in plaid perpendicular lines of hunter green and tawny brown. Over his aqua blue shirt he sported a tweed jacket of vermillion red and, for added panache, a flat brown ivy cap and a polka dot bow tie completed the ensemble. The business of his outfit made it difficult to maintain eye contact with his brown inquisitive eyes set in an otherwise plain pale face.

"Great. Michael. You don't mind if we dive right in then?"

"Please be my guest."

"A lot of people already say you've already reached the top — and at such a young age."

"Flattered," I replied with a smirk.

"So if I asked you if your best days were still ahead, what would you say to that?"

"Absolutely," I answered right away, not wanting to betray a subtle, yet gnawing vacancy I knew had slowly crept into my life. I was exhausted doing what I loved while living in a coveted dream.

I knew something was wrong, but could not begin to understand it so I carried on in the hope that if I ignored this sense, it would eventually go away. Seeming satisfied with my response, Paul moved on — and I silently exhaled in relief.

"Michael, most people out there who know you are already familiar with your background. There's dozens of articles out there with the same regurgitated story. I'm here because our readers want to know more about the man behind the music," Paul started. I winced at the speed in which he bypassed the details lining my protective outer shell, going instead straight for the soft underbelly like a hungry predator with no time to play. I reminded myself that this man was just doing his job and brushed off the assault with a chuckle.

"There's not much more than that to tell I'm afraid," I said, offering up a weak lie I knew would do nothing to deter him. "Music has just always been there. It was the only thing in life I could always count on."

As soon as the words were out, an involuntary flood of recall invaded my mind's eye, momentarily blinding me from the present scene in my office. I was back in the kitchen as a little boy looking into my dad's eyes as he hugged me and said, *"Oh buddy, I'll be right back before you know it. I'm not going anywhere."* His death turned his words into lies — words I couldn't count on.

And then there was the voice. The familiar echo filled my thoughts with the words which would haunt me at night as I wrestled to resist the reality of the moment when I first heard them as a young boy: *"I will never leave you. I will never forsake you."* These were the sleepless nights I found myself at war with the faith I once had and now declared to be false. I had long ago renounced the God who had spoken these words, but could not escape their resounding echo on the nights they crashed over me like waves, soaking my bedsheets in sweat.

A sudden sharp pain in my head accompanied the memories and grew stronger even as they faded from view and my office reappeared in my periphery. I pinched my temple and closed my eyes, letting out a groan.

"Michael, are… are you okay? You just suddenly went a bit pale there." Paul leaned forward in his chair, a concerned look crossing his face.

"Yeah, I'm fine," I said, still pinching my temple. "It's these damn headaches you know? I get them from time to time," I lied. Don't worry about it. Go on."

I reached into my top drawer and grabbed an Aspirin bottle and popped some of the pills in my mouth as Paul re-adjusted himself in his seat and carried on.

"Um, yeah. What I was getting at is, there's got to be more to the story than you've always just been really good at music. I mean, can you tell me what the source of inspiration is behind your songs?"

"What do you mean?" I asked, while searching frantically for anything to say that made sense besides a bunch of singing trees.

"Well, your songs—they have created some of the most beautiful sounds audiences have ever heard come from the stage. You can't tell me something like that just comes from nowhere. What do you believe to be the source of this sound? Do you meditate? Do you believe in God?"

"No!" I yelled, slamming my hand down with a bang.

My sudden and aggressive response shocked us both. My office fell silent except for a piercing ring in my ears which hit me like a concussion after my outburst. I grabbed my head and tried to recover the moment as another wave of pain rolled through.

"No… I do not believe in God. I simply write the music as I…. ahh!" The pain in my head intensified accompanied with a sudden wave of nausea. Not wanting to regurgitate my bagel from breakfast all over the recorder on my desk, I stood up and started walking for the door.

"I'm so sorry Paul; I don't know what's come over me. I'm afraid we're going to have to reschedule for another time. Be sure to talk with Debbie at the front desk on your way out. She's got your tickets and backstage passes for tonight's concert."

I said the words quickly and stepped out of my office and into the hall before Paul could even stand up from his chair. I didn't even look back before I stepped out of sight. I ran towards the washroom as my head continued to pound and the acidic taste of bagel constricted in my throat.

The musicians started to file in after lunch to set up their instruments. There was a wide array of age, experience, and accolades that filled the stage of the concert hall. Every one of them was a master in music and held my greatest respect and love — and I held theirs. But no matter where we all came from, the love for music made us a family. Every moment we played together was a moment we filled the atmosphere with a sound that found its source at the very depth of our souls.

I was feeling better now. The headache and nausea subsided after laying on the couch in the dark of my office for a while. I pushed all thoughts from the interview down into the recesses of my subconscious and focused on the pieces we would be performing tonight.

The concert started at seven-thirty in front of a full house. The evening's program was a tribute to young composers and their greatest works. Both Mozart and I had symphony pieces on the set list, along with other well-known composers in between. An article in the *New York Times* that morning touted the concert by drawing parallels between the young Amadeus and me. It was actually quite the flattering editorial, which would have eventually found its way into my scrap book, and certainly my mother's. But I had stopped collecting clippings from articles and publications for a while now. They had become like a gourmet fillet mignon to someone who had lost the sense of taste.

I stood to the side of the stage and watched the dispersion of light develop from a sliver to a luminous waterfall washing the orchestra as the curtain slowly opened. In the mornings when the concert hall was empty, I would walk to the center of the stage and stare out, absorbing my surroundings in quiet veneration. My footsteps on the hardwood would reverberate in the great room like the pounding of a pile driver in the still of the morning resonating against a mountain miles away. As I walked to the podium that evening, my footsteps could not be heard over the roar and applause from the audience. I walked through the rows of my standing ensemble and took my place with a bow. At the first stroke of my baton, our sound met with the anticipation of the audience like an electrical current when metal connects. The ebb and flow of the music were like sixty foot swells of sound which would collapse into the hush of a clear glass sea at my slightest gesture. These were the moments that I lived for. But before Mozart's Symphony No. 40 in G minor came to an end, my head was flooded with an intense searing pain that made the theatre go dark. I had already blacked out before I collapsed on the stage.

Chapter 7: Blake Fender

Blake Fender stood in line outside the New York Symphony Orchestra. *I wonder if anyone is going to recognize me here*, he thought to himself sarcastically with a quiet chuckle. He certainly stood out among the array of three-piece suits and evening gowns accented with priceless jewelry — but if anyone stared, it wasn't out of familiarity. He wore his "Sunday Best" but in Blake's church, that implied a sport jacket over a t-shirt accompanied with jeans and sneakers. The odd stare from those around didn't bother Blake. He carried a confidence that came from a healthy love for himself.

If anyone in the audience that evening did happen to recognize him, they were most likely going to be from his church, where Blake led Sunday morning worship with his guitar. Blake was a musician and like most of the others in line, he was there for the love of the music. But he was nothing like them. The other places he could have been seen within the city were far less likely to draw the same kind of audience.

On most Tuesdays, Blake would bring his guitar to Mount Sinai hospital and play for patients in various wards where he was welcome. It helped that one of his closest friends from church was also the hospital chaplain who often walked the halls with him. On Fridays and some Saturday nights, Blake could be found on a small stage in a pub or eatery, if he was lucky. Most of the time though, he would just have to find a spot in the corner of the bar where he could cram a microphone, a speaker, and a stool for him to perform.

Blake Fender was just another name on a corkboard poster in the vestibule of a bar. Other times he was only announced as "Live Music Tonight" on a sandwich board outside. Once again, it didn't bother Blake that he was just an unfamiliar name in a sea of obscurity, trying to amplify his sound in one of the largest cities in the world. Blake Fender wasn't even his real name. His driver's license and other pieces of identification revealed his young African American face and read: Kyle Thornton. Male. Age 24. Height 5'11." Eyes brown. Hair black.

Kyle didn't perform night after thankless night from a desire to one day be famous like most others chasing a dream — but a stage name, especially with the last name Thornton, certainly helped his chances of being heard at all. Though Kyle loved his church and saw it as his chance to connect the beating and often battered hearts of his congregation with the heart of his loving God, if he stayed confined within the church walls for too long he would stagnate into lethargy.

His greatest reward was often felt through the smiles and the tears of patients lying in their hospital beds, some of them knowing that they would never leave them. A church service was great, but it paled in comparison to catching a glimpse of moisture in the eyes of a lonely man drinking his beer in the corner of the bar. Those moments occurred often whenever Kyle wrapped up his set, as he always did, with a soulish rendition of "Amazing Grace." Those were the moments he lived for.

The crowd began filing into the amphitheater. There was no sweetheart on Kyle's arm. It was a Thursday evening and he was going alone. There were probably over a dozen single girls in his church who would have given an appendage to go on a date with him, but none of them pulled at his heart. He didn't feel the need to lead any of them along while he waited to meet the right one. Kyle navigated through the crowd, found his seat early, and settled in.

The orchestra was already positioned and meticulously tuning their instruments while making final adjustments to their seats and stands so that they could be comfortable for the evening. Kyle loved the acoustics in the great hall and enjoyed listening to the reverberation of sound from the warmup almost as much as from the music itself. It was the array of uncoordinated sonance of the instruments, combined with the anticipation and knowledge that they would immediately come together and find their stride the moment the conductor raised his baton for the first time. When Michael Mann finally walked onto the stage, the instruments stopped and everyone in the theatre rose to their feet in a symphony of applause that resonated within the walls of the concert hall.

The conductor acknowledged the audience and his waiting orchestra with a series of bows and gestures as the applause continued. Everyone slowly took their seats as the conductor faced his orchestra. Michael Mann lifted his baton and suspended it for the last silent moment of the night, which filled the room in pregnant anticipation of the sounds to follow. As the baton dropped there was a shift in the room as a crash of orchestrated harmonies collided with the silence. The concert had begun.

Kyle settled back into his seat and closed his eyes while the sound enveloped his senses. It was thrilling to watch the passionate violence of the conductor waving his arms through a *vivacissimo* transition with a single graceful gesture through a *lentando* in the musical piece. But with his eyes closed, he felt that he could hear the very heartbeat of the sound pulsing between heaven and earth. The music lifted Kyle out of his seat until he felt as though he was being carried by the sound suspended in the air. But in a single moment, Kyle came crashing to the ground as the jarring sound of the orchestra fumbling into an uneasy silence broke his trance.

When he opened his eyes, Michael Mann lay unconscious on the floor.

Part II

Chapter 8: Standing in Heaven

I awoke in darkness. Besides an awareness of myself, there was no point of reference as to where or what I was. A tranquil stillness enveloped me like a mother's womb, yet not so much as the subdued pulse of a heartbeat could be heard. I had been dropped into a void where the intangible was the substance of my surroundings, like an empty canvas untouched by the brush of matter. Had a thousand lifetimes passed, I would not have grown restless or fatigued. The placid space was marked with an absence of time. Wherever I was, I did not wait or grow old. I could not tell if I was flesh or soul. I could not tell if I walked, ran, or slept in the valley of the shadow that covered me.

I heard the music first before the light appeared, its sound immediately stirring a distant reminiscence. It was an artistic tapestry of ethereal harmonies woven with the terrestrial hails from nature. The wind in the trees, flowing streams, and the call from countless creatures blended in a dance of inflection and melodious cadence. It was both music and sound held together with rich tones that resonated in my soul—deep places I had retreated from and long forgotten about. Though I could not hear or even perceive if there were words in the music, a familiar narration echoed within the rhythm like the message of a timeless story.

A faint light dilated into view like an illuminated cloud of mist and progressively developed into an expanse of elevated radiance. The intensifying glow was blinding, but my eyes did not strain, nor could I turn away from its glory. The music emanated from the light in brilliant cascades of bright crescendo, but I could not distinguish the music from the light any more than I could discern the separation of water and sky while staring into the horizon across an ocean. It was slowly surrounding me with its melodious glow until my metamorphosis out of darkness was complete.

The impression of my surroundings in a graduated moment became unmistakably pronounced. I was standing in a meadow with a scattering of trees breaking up the rolling expanse of pristine hillside. The feel of lush grass below my feet alerted me to an awareness of my form. My feet! I had a body after all. But it was new and incorruptible and I was dressed in a full-length linen robe which hung elegantly on me like the embrace of a king.

Then I perceived with my eyes what my ears had been hearing, like stepping into the daylight from the depths of a dark cave. I looked all around and could see that the source of the music was not the light itself. All throughout the meadow I was surrounded by a great choir in the midst of a performance which I had attended before in the visions of my earliest memory. Rising all around me like great choral columns were the trees of various variety and age. A tremor of emotion coursed through me as I took in the sight which had changed me as a little boy and validated my earliest inspiration and assertion. It was the trees — and they were singing!

The chorus was new. I had never heard such a composition. Though its meaning remained hidden from me, I recognized throughout the song a familiar strain like strokes of a brush revealing the identity of the artist on a fresh canvas. The volume was not overpowering, but washed over me like a summer rainfall. I could feel the song engaging all of my senses. Light burst out of the trees along with their sound, which I could see dancing in a beautiful exchange with the wind like leaves caught up in the light spiral gust of a wind tunnel. The sound had a delicious taste like sweet bread, and its smell was fragrant like the balm of floral blossoms. I could feel it all around me like the refreshing water of a river carrying me downstream on its steady current.

And then I saw him. Just a short distance away, sitting on the stump of an ancient tree, was a man clothed in a simple white robe. His white hair shone with a glowing splendor and fell serenely to his shoulders. A white beard covered his face, but could not hide the captivating grace and brilliance emanating from it. His feet were bare and radiated with a bronze glow. And he was singing.

From deep inside of him came a melody reaching the far edges of the horizon with the valiancy of an arrow. His song was the overriding herald which brought every other note and accompanying harmony together in consonance with divine calculation and design. Though every other creature and sound was unique in its expression, this was the cry which rallied it all together and I discerned this One to be the true source of the music I was experiencing.

My heart leapt with involuntary wonder as my mind struggled to catch up to the magnitude of what I was experiencing. Long ago I had discredited the existence of God and walked away from faith just as naturally as I had embraced it when I was young. Pain and disappointment became the reality I could be sure of, while the idea of God faded into forgotten fable. But now, as I stood in stunned silence, there could be no doubt that I was in the presence of God.

He did not look directly at me, though I knew he saw me. His attention instead was fixed upon a little girl who sat in the meadow grass before him. The girl looked like she could not have been more than five years old, though I felt she had lived in this eternal place for ages where time had not yet touched her. The girl held Father

God's full attention and he looked deep into her eyes as he sang the song to her. She sat contently, smiling up at his face while the song washed over her like gentle rain.

It felt as though years could have passed as I stood in silent witness of the exchange taking place right before me. I could have easily remained in the moment forever as I felt my heart fill with an overflow of love, spilling out the sides of an already full cup. It was unmistakable. Though I had stopped singing the songs long ago, this was the love so many had written about that flowed from the Father heart of God.

I didn't notice when the Father stopped singing. The song continued to emanate from him though his lips were no longer moving. He continued to look intently down into the little girl's eyes as he spoke.

"It's time to go, my child," he said in a gentle tone.

"I know. I'm excited, but I want to stay here with you, Father," the girl responded without breaking from his gaze.

"My child, where you are going, I will always be with you and I will always be singing my song. Whenever you feel afraid or cannot see through the darkness, listen for my song. I will always be singing it over you," he said with a loving confidence.

"I will Father. I love you." The little girl stood up and embraced the Father as he knelt down to wrap his arms around her.

"I love you always, my child."

The Father remained kneeling on the ground though the girl was no longer there. She disappeared, as though she had been absorbed into His embrace. After a long pause the Father opened his hand to reveal a small seed resting in his palm. The Father started to sing again as he stood and turned back towards the large stump where he had been sitting. Leaning over with his open hand, he let the seed gently fall into the textured rings on the surface of the stump and then covered it with his hand like a parent tucking his child under warm blankets at night. He remained there with his hand covering the seed while his song seemed to wash over it like refreshing spring water.

"I love you, my child," he whispered his eyes fixed on the place where the seed had fallen. The Father then stood and started to slowly walk away. After a few steps, he stopped and paused. Without looking in my direction, he spoke to me for the first time. "I love that child so much. She will have difficulties where she is going, but she will always have my song to guide her if she will hear it."

He continued. "I've been looking forward to this time for longer than you know." He then turned around and faced me. My heart was immediately caught up by His deep and piercing eyes that held universes within them, yet conveyed a fierce love for me. "Come with me. I have much I want you to see and know." He said stretching his hand towards me.

As I walked towards him I looked back at the stump and could no longer see the seed sitting on its surface, but knew that it had begun to germinate deep inside the ancient roots.

Chapter 9: The Hospital

The ICU at Mount Sinai Hospital was a place that never slept. Its corridors were filled with a never-ending din of subtle beeps, alarms, and hushed conversations that continued well into the night. In one moment, the Father and I had been walking side by side through the serenade of meadow music and the very next found ourselves journeying down a corridor at Mount Sinai Hospital. The Father led as we navigated the wide yet congested hallways, past room after room which held a patient fighting for life in one way or another.

The Father approached room 132 at the end of the corridor and walked in. As I followed him to the threshold, a foreboding sense came over me, as one might get approaching a dead body for the first time at an open-casket memorial. As I entered the room it was clear why I felt that way. Lying in the bed in this room, buried under a complex tangle of hoses, tubes and wires — was me.

It was a shock to see myself lying there. An urge to turn around and leave started growing inside as I took in the spectacle of my body whose pallid complexion and lifeless frame reflected only a shadow of the man I used to be. But the Father remained standing at the foot of the bed in silence, so I held my ground at his side and started to take in the rest of the room. There were machines on both sides of my bed, monitoring, pumping, feeding, extracting, and breathing for my uninhabited body.

A young nurse busied herself at my bedside, fully absorbed in the checklists and routines that sustained life. Her blonde hair was tied back in a plain ponytail which bobbed back and forth just below her shoulders. She looked to be in her mid-twenties. Hidden beneath the features of her young and beautiful countenance, I could sense a sincerely sensitive and kind soul. It struck me that she wore no ring on her left hand as it seemed curious that a girl of her beauty could still be single. Around her neck she wore a stethoscope and an I.D. name badge. Her name was Kate Wylder.

Sitting off to one side in a chair was my wife. I did not see her there right away; her face was buried in her hands. I could tell by the stains on her cheek that she had been crying not very long ago — a thought that somehow warmed my heart, even if only mildly. In a chair next to her, a doctor sat and was talking. He held a clipboard loosely in his hands and referenced its notes often as he spoke in calming and compassionate tones.

"Your husband has suffered from a severe aneurism. From what our preliminary tests have shown, it has done some significant damage to his brain. As you know, we've done what we can to reduce the harm from initial swelling, but we won't know the full extent of his condition for some time. What is unusual about this is how suddenly it happened — and to a healthy man at such a young age. As far as you know, he didn't suffer from migraines or complain about headaches?"

"No," Jess sniffled. "We haven't been talking much lately. He's often gone to his concert hall early in the morning and sometimes he doesn't get back until well past midnight."

"I see," the doctor said. "And when was the last time you spoke with him?"

"Last night at bedtime. We were both listening to music in bed together after dinner and eventually said goodnight and went to sleep. He seemed fine."

Ha! *Something like that*, I thought to myself as the events of that evening flashed through my memory and I saw, once again, the broken vase and scattered flowers littering the floor.

There was a pause in the conversation as though the words forming in the doctor's mind had to be carefully crafted.

"We are going to remain optimistic and continue doing everything we can while we monitor Michael's progress, but the chances of him walking out of here as the same man you remember may not be a realistic expectation." The doctor stood, dropped his clipboard to his side and turned to look at Jessie. He was getting ready to leave and didn't need his notes anymore. "It was a really bad bleed and the swelling was substantial. He is going to be here for a long time. I'm talking probably months. If he does wake up, there is still no telling what kind of impact the trauma of the aneurism may have had on his capacity for the long term."

The doctor's shoulders lifted as he took a deep breath and exhaled. Although he spoke with a practiced balance of compassion and professionalism from having these conversations all the time, his sensitive delivery revealed an awareness that his words were nonetheless difficult to hear. "I'm so sorry that this is not the kind of news you want to hear, but we are not contributing to the success of his recovery if we can't be honest about where we are and where we are most likely headed."

There were no more tears from Jess at this point. Just a blank stare that conveyed a numbness as she processed the words now battering the façade of her perfect storybook life.

"Thank you doctor," she said without moving or breaking her stare at the floor.

"I'm very sorry," he said, and quietly left the room.

Kate Wylder had been at my bedside for the entire conversation, benevolently working away. Her voice broke the silence next after another long interval where my hospital machines were the only ones making any sound. "I'm so sorr-"

"Shut up!" Jessie snapped violently like a viper roused from its nest. "You don't know anything you stupid bitch!" Continuing now in her abrupt flash of rage, she turned her vehemence upon my lifeless body. "This is just like you to ruin everything! I hope you die!" She screamed.

With that, she quickly grabbed her purse and ran out of the room, fresh tears liberally cresting the reservoir of her emotions once again.

Kate froze lifelessly, completely suspended in the shock of the moment. Though I had encountered these eruptions plenty of times before, I too was left open mouthed and wide eyed from the sudden outburst. Another storm of the soul.

Kate had been yelled at by various family members visiting their loved ones in this hospital before. Unfortunately, unpredictable and high emotion from people watching their loved ones suffer or die could be just as common as gushy gratitude and over-the-top admiration. They were the two extremes that manifested in the private I.C.U. rooms on a regular basis. Nurses and staff could never know which one was going to get dragged in with their patient. Either way it took its toll.

Slowly, Kate started to move again as the immediate impact from the encounter began to wear off, like the echoing percussion from a gunshot fading across a wide open field. She grabbed a fresh I.V. bag and started to replace one hanging on a busy tree of hooks when the Father started to slowly walk across the room towards her.

He had been standing right beside me the entire time. Still. Calm. The sound of his song was always there, subtly emanating out of him like oxygen from a living tree. He did not flinch at Jess's outburst, nor was he jarred by the doctor's report. His presence held the integrity of the room together though the very walls were threatening to burst apart, shaken like an earthquake by the buffeting volatility of life.

The Father walked up to Kate until he stood close beside her, almost touching. Kate continued about her task completely unaware of the Father standing so close. He stood and watched her work for a time. Then he leaned in and spoke softly into to her ear.

"My daughter. This man will make a full recovery."

Kate froze again suddenly at the words as though in shock. The empty I.V. bag, rocking back and forth slowly in her hands, was the only observable movement. It was obvious that although she had been unaware of our presence until this moment, she heard the Father's words which now resonated in the quiet of her heart and the room.

The Father walked back to his spot beside me as Kate began to slowly thaw from her brush with the divine. She took a few steps around to the other side of the room, her eyes still fixed and unblinking. She fell into one of the chairs where Jess and the doctor had sat moments ago and remained there for a long time, the I.V. bag still dangling from her hand. The Father, satisfied that His words had landed, turned to me.

"Come, there is something else I want to show you," he said.

The Father led me through crowded corridors and spacious atriums of the hospital until we found ourselves in the maternity ward. As soon as we crossed through the main nursing station I was struck with the dynamic dichotomy between the ICU and the place where we now stood. There was a vibrancy in the environment that could not be felt on the other wards, almost as though the very song of heaven I had been immersed in had penetrated the veil of humanity in this place and remained subtle but ever present like a pulse. The hallways popped in a smattering of color from the various displays of art that decorated the walls and in place of stretchers and hospital beds were small infant-sized nursery beds no larger than a few shoe boxes put together. The Father found the open door for the room and disappeared behind the curtain separating it from the hall. I followed.

The private room was full of people. I quickly observed that in this small space there were two nurses, two doctors, and a man visibly fatigued and dressed in plain, comfortable clothes. Holding all of their attention, laid out on the bed, was a mother coming to the end of her labor. The haggard-looking man, obviously the husband and soon-to-be father held on to his wife's hand while she rested. Her eyes were closed, and she was breathing heavily and lying on bedsheets drenched in sweat. Layered on top of the constant sounds of monitors, the clatter from nurses preparing more tools and equipment and the doctors articulating in medical language, was the constant chorus of encouragement from the husband and the medical staff.

"I'm so done. I don't want to do this anymore. I can't. I can't. I can't," the woman moaned through her heavy breathing. Tears broke through the woman's closed eyes, adding to the profusion of moisture pouring out of her pores and soaking her sheets.

One of the nurses interjected with calm reassurance. "You've got one more big push and this baby is here, sweetie. When you feel it coming I want you to give it one last push with all you've got. You can do this."

"You hear that, baby? We're almost there. You've got this. I'm so proud of you," the husband said, drawing from his own exhausted reserves of lent strength.

A sudden cry of pain from the woman and euphonic cheers from everyone in the room blended with another voice joining the noise as a little baby girl made her screaming entrance into the world. The child was received into a bed of gloved hands that worked quickly to wipe the afterbirth of the womb from her face and body. The pediatrician cut the cord and sucked residual fluid from baby's mouth, which was hardly enough to stifle her little cry as air filled her lungs for the first time.

While all of this activity seemed to cascade into the room at once, I was caught up in my own moment of awe which halted time once again and left me speechless. Above the cacophony of the moment I could hear heaven's song breaking into the room like someone had opened a door to a great concert hall infusing the atrium with sound. The music at first appeared to be coming from the woman's womb, but as the baby passed through from life inside her mom to life outside, the sound followed and emanated from her tiny body like a glow from the Northern Lights. While the doctors and nurses quickly worked to clean and swaddle the child, I stood and listened while I beheld the sight. The song I heard so clearly in heaven and subtly in the corridors of the maternity ward now flowed from the baby girl like a spring. I could hear the music loud and clear above her little cry.

I looked at the Father to find that he was already looking at me with a smile. We didn't speak at first, but exchanged within the moment of our glance were the words that answered the questions of my heart.

"You have seen this child not long ago as she disappeared into my embrace," he said.

"Is she…?" I started to ask before my words trailed off.

"Yes, this is the girl you saw in the meadow and she has now come into her life in this place. My song can still be heard from inside of her. I put it there and it will never leave though over time it will come to fade. This child will have difficulties here, but I will never stop singing my song over her. If she will hear the sound of heaven and recognize my song, she will remember who she is and where she has come from. She is my child whom I love. She has come into this world to introduce another facet of my joy and love which has never been seen before; and she will do it with the help of my song.

The Father returned his gaze upon the small child now swaddled in blankets and nestled in her mother's embrace. Hot tears streamed down the woman's face who now held in her hands for the first time the life she had long been carrying. Her joyous outbursts of laughter broke through her sobs. The proud dad covered his two girls like a bird's wing while a tear fell from his chin and mixed with the sweat in his wife's tangled hair. It was the most beautiful mess one could ever behold on this earth.

The doctors and nurses continued to work and monitor from a distance while the family stayed nestled together in their moment — oblivious to the activity around them and the music that filled the room from their daughter's song.

The Father lingered in the moment while I continued to process the events of the last few hours — which, for all I knew, could have been another lifetime in heaven. It was not until all was quiet in the little room that the Father approached me again.

The mother had fallen asleep with her little girl resting in her arms. The dad, now asleep as well, lay curled on a small bench that folded out as a bed and a single nurse hovered over an I.V. tree in the corner of the room. The quiet scratches from her pen as she took notes on her chart were the only sounds in the room.

"It is time now to come with me, I have much more to show you," the Father said.

Kate walked to her car in the hospital staff parking lot, exhausted from the work and emotions of the day — more so from this day than any other. The outburst from Jessie continued to flash across her mind and cause her heartrate to increase each time. It may happen all the time, she thought, but that didn't make it any easier for the nurses on the receiving end.

She walked up to her car door, opened it, and sat down inside. When the car door closed and there was silence for the first time in twelve hours, Kate heard the echo of the voice that spoke to her heart. Whether it had been an audible voice or not, she could not tell. It was that clear. There were two statements now repeating through her head.

"This man will make a full recovery..."

Kate had seen a lot of people come back from the brink of death in her experience, but this seemed to come at her the same day she heard doctors pronounce the very opposite outcome. The arguments between her faith and her knowledge clashed somewhere between her head and her heart. But then there was the other statement.

"My daughter..."

Kate had grown up in the church all her life. She attended a small Baptist congregation outside of town and knew her Bible well.

82

Of course she knew that God loved her. Of course Jesus died for her sins… Of course, of course, of course. But it seemed now for the first time in her life that these two words from the Father travelled the eighteen-inch journey from her head and collided with her heart, breaking a dam that had been sealed up over a lifetime.

'My daughter,' she thought.

The divine epiphany washed over her like a wave and shattered the brass ceiling suspended between her and heaven. She saw herself as a child in the loving arms of Father God and her heart swelled as a healing balm filled it to overflowing. Her drive that evening was slower than usual as she had to negotiate her way through the blurred vision of her tears as she wept the entire way home.

Chapter 10: The Winking Judge

The Winking Judge was a well-known establishment in the East side of the city, one block away from the district court house. It attracted a steady stream of business-casual throughout each work day from the offices all around, and in the evenings the scene would transform to reflect the diverse tapestry of the city and many of the young working class who called it home. There was a small corner of the room where the owner had set up a platform barely large enough to accommodate a single stool and a mic stand where Blake Fender was setting up for the Friday night crowd.

The Winking Judge was one of his more liked venues for the simple reason that the owner did not have a smattering of T.V. screens peppering the walls where a thousand images could distract his patrons from the individual souls sharing the room with them. Blake often had to endure evenings when he felt as though he played to himself while the small crowd in the room fixed their attention on the sports game or the news. That was all fine to him. He had already committed himself to playing for an audience of One no matter where he went. Still, he enjoyed looking into the faces of the crowd when he had the chance. Those were his favorite nights.

As he set up his small stage area he thought about the conductor, Michael Mann and his collapse. He couldn't get the scenes from last night's events out of his head as they seemed to play through his mind on a recurring loop. What an awful, gut-wrenching moment when the orchestra came to a stumbling halt, colliding with the collective gasp of the crowd as Michael hit the stage floor. Some of the crowd were on their feet immediately, but then froze in place just as fast, unsure of what to do next. It took a few awkward moments before the stage curtain began to move. Some of the violinists were at the conductor's side and a stage hand took off running by the time the curtains sealed the scene from the audiences view. Canned music came on in the system overhead as the house lights illuminated the great hall which helped mute the panicking voices from the cluster of stage hands and musicians huddled around their conductor.

A man dressed in a suit approached the front of the stage in front of the curtain and tried his best to make an announcement without a microphone or any idea what to say. He tried to project as loud as he could though the panic was evident in his voice as well. The audience was asked to calmly make their way out of the auditorium through the side exits leaving the center isle clear for the first responders who were already on their way. Slowly the crowd began to disperse along the side isles. The sound of the approaching sirens in the distance could already be heard above the din of the dispersing crowd and house music.

Blake Fender opened his guitar case revealing the beautiful old acoustic Fender inside.

"Hello Grandpa. Are we ready to sing tonight?" Blake addressed his guitar as he lifted it and attached the strap to the post. "Grandpa" was the name he affectionately bestowed upon his guitar. Blake's grandpa gave the guitar to him before he passed away and before Kyle Thornton inherited his stage name. "Gramps" Thornton was a true musician who could pull tunes from that instrument to fit any genre of music at the drop of a hat, though his love language was gospel and blues. Although Kyle Thornton experienced healthy and loving relationships with his parents, his grandpa was the brightest star in his young life. It was Gramps who taught Kyle how to play the guitar and on his ninth birthday, Gramps gave him his first: a Mini Taylor. Because his grandpa lived in a house across the street, Kyle could disappear and jam for hours without worrying his parents much.

Those sessions endured through six wonderful changings of the seasons where Kyle mastered his art under the mentoring and guidance from his best friend. Those were the best years of Kyle's life. When Kyle was fifteen, Gramps collapsed from a heart failure and was rushed to the hospital where the medical staff were able to bring him back from the brink of death. Kyle was in school when he got the news and got a ride to the hospital with one of the teachers who could hardly say no to his desperate and tearful plea. He sobbed silently in the car the entire drive across town and when he got to the hospital, broke into a run, his tears still hitting him in waves as he called out for directions to hospital staff without slowing his pace.

He didn't check in at the nurses' station or ask for permission to burst into his grandfather's room. As he stepped in, he paused long enough to catch his breath and take in the scene. Gramps lay sitting up in his bed, more tired and pale than Kyle had ever seen him before, but awake and in good spirits. He was talking quietly with a nurse who was busy changing out an I.V. bag when he saw Kyle step in the room.

"Hey there, kiddo," Gramps said, regarding his grandson with a reassuring smile.

Kyle launched himself at his grandfather's bed and threw his arms around him. There were no words while a liberal flow of tears ran its course through Kyle and soaked into the hospital bedsheets.

The nurse fidgeted with the I.V. bag for a few awkward moments before leaving the room and closing the door behind her.

Gramps stayed in the hospital under observation before transferring to a quieter ward as he was still too weak to care for himself. It became clear early in the process that Gramps recovery was more of a postponement to the inevitable. He could count on visits from Kyle once or even a few times a day during the weeks he stayed in care. Gramps couldn't play anymore himself so Kyle would bring one of his guitars from his growing collection and play for his grandpa for hours. In the few short weeks that this went on for, the young lad with a guitar gained a reputation among the patrons up and down the halls of the ward and was eventually asked to play for others who could hear his music percolating through the thin walls of their rooms — the humble beginnings of his future hospital outreach.

One of those days a few weeks into his stay, Gramps turned to his grandson and said, "Bring me my guitar when you come tomorrow, my boy."

The next day Kyle brought his grandpa's old Fender to the hospital. It had the endearing name "Gramps" scratched on the back of the body.

"Play something for me on that ol' girl, son," Grandpa said with noticeable frailty in his voice.

Kyle quickly gave it a tune and started to skillfully pluck the melody of what he knew was grandpa's favorite song: "Amazing Grace." Gramps closed his eyes and listened as the tune washed over him. When the song came to an end no one spoke for a while. Then, after a long pause, Gramps turned to Kyle.

"That was beautiful." There was moisture in his eyes as he spoke. "Son, will you take care of my ol' girl for me? I think it's time

87

that I passed her on to you."

"What? No Grandpa! She's yours and you're going to get better and we're going to play together some more."

A swell began to develop in Kyle's eyes and pinch his throat as he protested. Grandpa didn't respond back and let the silence do the talking for him as he gazed affectionately into the eyes of his only grandson.

Gramps finally spoke again after a long moment of silence.

"Do you remember what I taught you about the song inside your heart? The one that only you can play in this world?" Gramps asked reminiscently.

"Yes. You tell me all the time, Grandpa," Kyle said with a sniffle.

"I think that ol' girl is going to help you find that song of yours. You guys need each other now," he said.

"How am I going to know when I've found it? I don't even know where to look." Kyle questioned.

"Yes you do, my boy. Who created you in the first place?"

"God," Kyle replied, now wiping an eye and staring at his feet.

"God. God who?" Gramps plied.

"God the Father," Kyle responded weakly.

"Yeah. That's right. God *the Father*," Gramps replied with some strength returning to his voice. Gramps continued, "And who loves you more than anyone else could possibly even fathom in this world?"

"God the Father," Kyle echoed, his eyes still fixed on the ground.

"God the Father. That's right. Kyle, look at me son."

Kyle lifted his head and fixed his gaze on his grandpa once

again.

"You're inside the Father's heart. He created you from that place with a song of love. Kyle, find the Father's heart and you'll find the song that you're meant to sing back to him. That's the reason we're here. There's no greater place to be than in the Father's heart of love. Once you're in that place, you'll find that once you start singing, the words, well, they'll just flow."

That was the last conversation Kyle had with his grandfather. Grandpa Thornton passed away in his sleep that night and Kyle woke up to the news which filled his life with an emptiness and broke his heart in pieces.

But Grandpa's words never left him. The seeds had been planted and over time Kyle learned to open up his heart and face his uncertainty and pain, despite a strong and natural urge to run and hide from it or medicate it away. His inclination towards honest dialogue and raw emotion in his times with God through the storms of life cultivated a strong faith and led him to a place of healing and wholeness. The Father was singing over Kyle and gradually he began to hear it resonate in his heart like a song on the radio emerging out of the static as a traveler gets closer to home.

Performing at the Winking Judge that evening, interspersed between Tom Petty, Johnny Cash, and John Lee Hooker, were songs that emerged from Kyle's heart which had come out of his times alone with God; and Blake Fender was performing them on grandpa's old guitar:

"All I have left to give is what has been through the fire
All I have left to live is who I am in you
You knew me from the very start
Before I knew your name

Your love broke through and claimed my heart
Which now is ever changed
Now I know beauty from ashes and grace for each day
I'm your breath of life and beating heart formed from the clay."

Throughout the night the crowd would ebb and flow between engagement and abstraction while Blake Fender performed. And, as always, to close off the song list for the evening, he played his arrangement of "amazing grace" in a soft mix of gospel and blues. And, as always, by the end of the song, he could pick out the glimmer of a tear rolling down the cheek of one or two members of the audience.

Chapter 11: Exposed

We were back in my apartment the very next moment standing in my bedroom. It felt as if I had only been there hours ago yet I could tell right away it had been a few days — or longer. There was a smattering of Jessie's yoga attire and skimpy underwear scattered across the floor. This was normal. I would regularly pick up after my wife and put her clothes in the laundry basket. I noticed the bed. It wasn't made and there were dirty wine glasses on both nightstands.

"We're in my bedroom. I thought you said we were going back to the meadow?" I said in a puzzled voice.

The Father looked at me and said, "We are going back to the meadow. This is the way we must go. There is still much to see and know."

I could hear commotion coming from our ensuite off the bedroom. The door was partially open and light spilled into the bedroom where it remained dark save for the glow coming from the kitchen down the hall. Jessie came out wrapped in a towel, running a comb through her damp hair. She started talking out loud which caught me off guard. I had never known her talk to herself before.

"I've been thinking about putting in my notice at the gym," she said casually, still brushing her hair.

Before I could process that statement as being odd to say out loud alone, I heard the voice of a man respond from inside the bathroom before he stepped into the room — fully naked.

"Why would you do that?" He asked drying his hair with a

small hand towel. I stood in the corner in complete bewilderment and cried out involuntarily at the top of my voice: "What?!"

The sound of my voice in the small room shocked me back to silence and I winced in expectation of being discovered. But nothing happened. No one heard my cry of outrage. Jessie continued in her casual tone.

"Well, I've been getting kind of bored teaching the same class over and over again. And I think they would understand me wanting to take some time off because of what I'm going through. You know, grieving wife stuff," she said with a hint of cynicism at the end.

"The guy's not that close to the end, is he?" The man asked. By "the guy" I figured he was referring to me and a flush of rage momentarily blinded my vision with images of me strangling this maggot of a man with my bare hands until his body stopped twitching. I felt the Father take a step towards me and hold my hand in his. The rage disappeared, but my heart continued to break apart while the scene played out in my bedroom before me.

"The doctor says that a full recovery doesn't seem that likely so I'm going to suggest that *my husband* probably wouldn't want to live in a world where he couldn't play his music. If things go the way I'm thinking, they'll probably pull the plug in a few more weeks." She emphasized 'my husband' in her remark, in a way that seemed to indicate she was subtly coming to my defense; although overall, the scene continued to invoke torment like brine on a festering wound.

The man grabbed the towel wrapped around my wife and whipped it to the floor and he pulled her into himself so that their damp naked bodies pressed together with a nauseating smack. I couldn't watch any longer and stared at the towel on the floor while they continued to talk.

"And where does that leave you?" The man asked. I could hear them start to kiss.

"Grieving..." some more kisses. "And rich," she said sardonically and drove the knife in deeper.

"And where does that leave us?" He continued. His breathing starting to get a bit heavier between kisses.

"Wherever the hell we want," my wife proclaimed with a giggle. I heard them both laugh and fall together into our bed.

I felt the squeeze of the Father's hand in mine. "There's more to see," he said, indicating, to my relief, that it was time to go.

I didn't know if I could handle any more. I was shattered and felt like crumbling on the floor— lying as limp and discarded as Jessie's towel. I knew I didn't want to see anything else that the Father had to show me, but I also knew that I didn't want to stay in my bedroom any longer while this scene played out. Fortunately, we left the room as my wife and the man stopped talking and their breathing grew heavier.

Chapter 12: Jessie's Pain

The Father and I stood in another bedroom. At first glance I could tell this one belonged to a little girl. The walls were painted a pastel pink. There was a full-sized doll house that reached halfway to the ceiling along one wall and pictures of birds and flowers were tastefully hung on the others. Judging by the size of the room and the fact that it had a walk in closet off to one side, it must have been a larger house in an affluent neighborhood.

A little girl who couldn't have been older than seven was playing quietly at the doll house. Her light blond hair was combed and fell in straight lines halfway down her back. She was wearing a light blue t-shirt that said *I Love Unicorns* and had a picture of a unicorn with a horn decorated in fuzzy textures intermingled with sparkling sequins. She wore pink corduroy shorts and wore nothing on her feet. She had a mom and a dad doll in each hand and in her little dollhouse world, they were both huddled around a crib tucking their baby in for a nap. She was singing a lullaby softly in the voice of the parents as they watched their child slowly drift off to sleep. I heard a sniff come from my side and turned to catch a tear rolling down the Father's cheek. I was startled to see him crying.

The Father turned and spoke in a soft and broken voice. "Son, you know this child but you don't know her pain. No one does except for me."

Just then from the open door of the bedroom behind me I heard a voice of a man that sent a chill through my body and felt a vile hostility cast a dark shadow over the natural light and wonder of the room.

"Hi Jessie. Whatcha doin' there little girl?" The man said. I turned towards the doorway and saw a smirk on his face that made the hair stand up on the back of my neck. The man looked to be in his early forties, Caucasian, clean shaven, and modern glasses with short styled hair. He must have come from work as he still wore a white shirt with a loosened red tie and grey dress pants. Based on his appearance alone one would not hesitate to trust this man with a mortgage or a venture capital investment on the spot. But now as he leaned on the frame of the bedroom doorway and looked in, a nausea twisted at my gut and I felt like a trapped animal in a dark alley while he barred my only escape.

Jessie was the little girl and the revelation broke through like a crushing avalanche that this was my wife and I must have been standing in her home where she grew up in a suburb just outside of LA. And the man—he must have been her step dad. I knew her real father left when she was only three and I knew she grew up with a step dad but never heard much about him—and I was starting to understand why.

I could feel my heartrate double as the full impact of this insight compounded with the looming nausea of the moment. Jessie hadn't moved when she heard the voice but froze with the dolls still in her hands overlooking the cradle. And then the words I spoke the last time we were together came rushing back in vivid memory. "Jess, it's like you're trying to live in a dollhouse where everything is always… perfect." Then smash went the vase—I had no idea.

I could feel the darkness in the room and could tell by how she tensed that she had the same poisonous bile churning in her stomach.

"Your mom's not going to be home for a while so she asked if I could make you dinner. Do you want me to make you your favorite?" The man asked with a carnal inflection and a sinister grin.

"No thanks," Jessie said softly. I could hear the fear in her voice. "I'm not hungry."

"Well darlin', you've got to eat something. It might as well be your favorite. I'm going to make you pancakes," he said with resolute inevitability.

If there's one thing I knew about my wife, it was that she hated pancakes. I remembered back to our honeymoon and the fateful morning at our resort when I first learned this about her. I got to the restaurant ahead of time and ordered breakfast for the both of us. It was pancakes. *Who doesn't like pancakes* I thought to myself. She got to the table and sat down for her coffee before the breakfast arrived. When the waiter delivered our meals and she saw pancakes stacked on our plates her storm rolled in and she erupted at the waiter and myself in a torrent of profanity before running from the restaurant back to our room where she hid for the rest of the day. I never ordered her breakfast again.

"I don't want pancakes. I'm not…"

"Don't you argue with your step-dad young lady." The man in the doorway snapped back at Jessie who still hadn't moved an inch from her spot.

"Now, if I'm going to do something nice for you you've got to do something nice for me. You know what your daddy likes," he continued slyly.

Jessie didn't move and my heart sunk into the digestive acid of my twisted insides.

"Young lady, don't make me tell your mom what a naughty girl

96

you've been. If you go now I promise this will still just be our little secret and no one has to find out."

Slowly Jessie stood up and started to take her shorts off out of resigned intimidation. She then walked towards the darkness of her open walk in closet never taking her eyes off the floor. Her dad stopped her again in her steps.

"Ah-ah. Underwear too darlin'. Don't make me ask you again," he said. I wanted to scream once again. I wanted to tear this man's throat out and watch him bleed. I wanted to leave this place and take Jessie with me but knew I couldn't.

Jessie stopped before reaching the closet and did what her father said before disappearing into darkness. A sinister cloak of satisfaction that only a predator can wear darkened the man's demeanor further still as he successfully wielded his power over his helpless victim once again. He stepped out from the doorway and walked into the closet and into the darkness of Jessie's recurring nightmare.

Mercifully, that was the last thing I saw. I had gone as well, journeying once again with the Father through the veiled dimension between time and space — hoping there was no more left to see and know.

Chapter 13: Trauma

The sounds, smells, and sensation of the armored transport leaving the ground as the improvised explosive device thrust it into the air with a concussive blast were at times still more real to First Lieutenant E. Bishop than his peaceful surroundings in military barracks where he now found himself serving back home. The screams of agony and terror could often and unexpectedly break through louder than a football game blaring from a big screen in a bar. The adrenaline from ambush gunfire that kept him pinned down while he watched his best friend bleed out yards away would still cause him to wake up in bedsheets soaked in his own sweat. As if that wasn't enough baggage for one man to carry, like kerosene on a dumpster fire, interspersed between his flashbacks from the theatre of active duty, he could still feel the sting from his dad's hand on the side of his face and taste the blood in his mouth from a time in his life before he could even grow facial hair. And now he had a child of his own.

The Father and I stood outside rows of housing that stretched in orderly columns under the shade of old growth trees which had been uniformly planted in orderly lines some years ago. The age of the houses could no longer remain hidden behind the layers of paint that held them together which suggested the trees stood only a few feet tall when they were first planted when the barracks were first built. A steady hum from a highway in the distance blended with the sound from air conditioning units fighting to keep each house below eighty degrees. Still the odd chirp from a songbird, and playful hollers from other kids in different areas of the compound were easily heard above the din of white noise. A few yards away from where we stood, a little boy played with toy soldiers and tanks in a small sandbox. The boy looked to be almost three years old.

There was a simplicity in the scene that I felt might not last. The Father was still 'showing me things' and from what little I had already experienced within these surreal surroundings, I was waiting for the serenity to dissipate. As if on cue, shouts were heard from inside the house in front of where the boy was playing. A man's voice was raging inside and a woman's voice, its tone defensive, was on the receiving end of the barrage. In the next instant, like an explosion from a cannon, the screen door swung open and slammed against the side of the house, before breaking off its hinges and falling to the ground from the impact. The shock startled the boy in the sandbox and he immediately began to cry.

The door's assailant, now outside, marched up to the sobbing child. The man wore standard issue military clothing. His calf-high boots kicked up dust from the ground, making an intimidating thump with each nearing step. He was a tall imposing figure who looked to be in his mid-thirties. His hair was cut short and his face clean shaven. He was handsome in his own way but for the broody scowl masking a sensitive soul which had not been exposed to the world in over two decades. As the man grabbed the boy violently and lifted him up by both arms the child gave out a scream of terror and the deterioration of the scene was in full nose dive with a fiery crash imminent. The man began shaking the boy who screamed more with every jarring tremor.

"Shut up, Travis! You're always crying! Why are you always crying?" The man yelled only inches away from the boy's face.

Just then the woman came bursting out of the broken doorway yelling and rushing to the boy.

"Leave him alone Eugene! Leave him alone and just get out of here!" She hollered in a panicked fury.

Lieutenant Bishop gave Travis one last jolt before dropping him in the sand where he crashed, and lay crumpled over like the wreckage of a downed plane. He stepped over his son and into a nearby car and roared away. The screech of tires left behind a patch of black and a cloud of smoke reeking of burnt rubber and gasoline. When the sound and the smoke dissipated, Eugene's casualties lay scattered and dazed like fallen soldiers in the aftermath of a grisly offensive.

Travis's mom picked him up and the boy huddled in his mother's arms still crying in weighty sobs. As I surveyed the scene, a sudden flash of insight occurred to me. The little boy, now a broken pile of tears wrapped in his mother's arms was the same boy who, in another time, would release his own similar and savage rage upon my precious violin, leaving me crumpled on the floor in the same broken and sobbing state. This little child was Travis Bishop, my high school bully.

The mother sat in the sand, rocking her child, staring blankly, as Travis continued to sob like a broken record between quick convulsing breaths. She looked numb and lost in her own thoughts. Her marriage lay in a contorted pile, as fractured as the screen door. Trapped. Scared. Exhausted with worry. It all showed itself in heavy dark lines under her eyes that creased an otherwise beautiful and young face.

I looked over at the Father. In that moment I wanted to say, 'I know that boy' but abruptly choked back words and fell silent as I observed the Father once again with tears in his eyes looking upon the mother and child. He stood arrested in their plight and pain and overflowing with empathy and compassion. The Father lifted one of his hands out in front of him and, as if on command, a single sparrow alighted on the side of the sandbox in front of Travis and his mom. They both saw the bird land and Travis's sobs receded down to short breaths as he became captivated by the little hopping creature who didn't seem bothered by his close proximity to the pair. The Father began to speak while not breaking his eyes away from the sandbox.

"Instead of pain, this child will know joy. One day he will realize I have been with him all along and he will give me his sorrows in exchange for something far better. The gifts I give to this child he will not be able to contain and they will spill out into the lives of many others. He doesn't know I am here with him now but I will redeem this moment a thousand times before his life is over," he said while tears flowed unreservedly down the side of his face.

The Father began to sing quietly while remaining fixed on the child and mother. It was the same song from the meadow and yet carried a distinct strain as unique as a fingerprint. He approached the sandbox and knelt over the two, embracing them in his arms like a hen covering her young babies. No one seemed intent on moving any time soon including the sparrow who was hopping around now only inches from the mother and child.

I heard the sound of a screen door close from behind me and turned to see another man approaching us carrying a small toolbox in his hands. The man had short red hair and was wearing the standard issue green t-shirt, pants and boots with his dog tags dangling around his chest. He didn't say anything as he walked right past the sandbox and up to the screen door on the ground. He picked it up and started to repair the hinges while the Father and the sparrow continued to sing to the mother and her child.

The contrasting sounds of the Father's song and the clatter from the drilling and hammering both carried the same redemptive strain in a blended dance of resonance. The screen door would never be new again, but the kindness that initiated its restoration would be a memory that would break through louder than the noise which delivered the damage. The repair took about twenty minutes and all the while, the scene in the sandbox remained unchanged and serene. When the screen door was fixed, the young soldier tested it a few times and was satisfied by the click it made when it closed. He packed the tools back up in his box and got a broom from inside the house and swept off the landing before finally walking over to the mother and child still nestled together. As soon as he got up to the sandbox, the sparrow, who had remained there the entire time, finally flew away. In the same moment, the Father returned to my side under the tree. The soldier bent down to acknowledge the child in his mother's arms as he addressed him.

"Hey there Travis, my little buddy. That was a pretty cool bird, wasn't it? I think he liked you. He didn't even move the whole time," the soldier said with compassionate enthusiasm.

Travis remained silent in his mom's embrace, but regarded the man with a shy smile. The soldier gave Travis a wink before turning his attention to his mother.

"Door's all fixed, Amy. It's not pretty, but it works." He let out a light, resigned chuckle.

"Thanks Nick," Amy said, still not moving from her place with her son.

"I'm sorry you had to go through that. Eugene's going through a tough time. We all are." As he said it, a blank stare glazed across

Nick's face and for a moment, he vanished into the same recurring nightmare of explosions, screams, gunfire, and death. Catching himself quickly, he returned to the present and spoke to Amy again. "I'll go and check on him a little later. Make sure he's okay."

Amy nodded and Nick stood once again and returned to his home across the lane.

When Nick had gone, the mother finally spoke to her son. "Come on Travis, let's go inside and get some supper." They both stood up and brushed the sand off as best as they could before returning back inside their house with the sound of a click from the screen door closing behind them.

I waited for a while for the Father to say something next, but he seemed content to remain still. I couldn't think of anything to say myself, but as I took that time to process what I had watched, I found myself being warmed with an awareness of compassion and empathy I had never experienced before. Part of me wanted to chase after the mom and her boy and give them both a big hug just as the Father had. I wanted to tell the little boy that everything was going to be okay. I thought about this for a while before finally breaking the silence.

"That poor little guy. I hope he's going to be alright."

The Father seemed to be content at that as though it had been the change of heart he had been waiting for.

"He will be," the Father said with a knowing smile and led us off once again into another familiar moment in time.

Chapter 14: Bad News

Some had to stand along the back of the wall as the small hospital meeting room exceeded its capacity. In the three weeks that Michael had been in a coma, almost all of the members of his family had managed to make their way to the Big City which their brother and son called home. His mom Helen was there within the first few days of the incident and had found a hotel to stay in close by. His twin sisters each had left their children back home on the West Coast with their husbands and made arrangements to stay with a mutual friend from college who now lived in New Jersey. Madeline, Michael's other sister, lived in New York like her brother and was attending an arts college on a scholarship. Her fiancé stood behind her chair with a somber stare which embodied the mood in the room reflected on the faces of all the others gathered around the small conference table. There were two members of the orchestra, a violinist and a trumpeter, who had befriended Michael in his earlier years before he settled in New York and were now the closest to extended family that he had nearby. They had been by Michael's bedside often over the course of the past many weeks.

Jessie sat with Brenda, one of the unit social workers, on one side of her, and the two doctors who had been overseeing Michael's care on her other side. She kept her stare fixed down at the table surface in front of her to avoid making eye contact with others in the room. Kate Wylder, who had become one of Michael's regular nurses, stood along the back wall in the room at the invitation of Michael's mother who had come to admire Kate for the quality care she was giving her son. Kate was not the only person Jessie had berated in the past few weeks — now half of the family members in the room could say that they found themselves on the receiving end of Jessie's unpredictable flairs. In one moment she could be calm and weepy, and in the next moment, she'd serve volleys of expletives to anyone attempting to infiltrate her world with compassion. By now, invisible lines from a silent standoff had been drawn around her periphery as most of the family chose to remain on their side of the line giving Jessie the distance that everyone now had grown comfortable with.

The stack of reports compressed by the clipboard holding them together appeared thinner than they actually were. In three weeks the tests, reports, and charts created quite the pile of paper with not one single sheet holding much information to support hope. The I.C.U. doctor stared at the reports in front of him while internally going through the familiar exercise of exchanging the medical terms for their vernacular equivalent. He had done this many times before with families, but that brought little comfort to the ones in the room now. No matter how he explained it, terms such as Pontine Hemorrhage and Intracranial Brain Atrophy were associated with a very poor prognosis. He spoke first.

"Hello everyone. For those of you who don't know me yet, my name is Dr. Morris. I've been one of Michael's doctors since he first arrived in our I.C.U. here at Mt. Zion. This is my colleague Dr. Wells. He is the neurosurgeon who led the initial surgical evacuation on Michael in an attempt to relieve the pressure from the hemorrhage in his brain. I think by now you all know Brenda as well, who's done an excellent job assisting where she can with the family's needs and we all know Kate who has been one of Michael's nurses and by now has become one of the trusted family friends in this place. Thank you all for being here today at the request of the family," Dr. Morris said with poignant professionalism.

There was a pause now as Dr. Morris shifted in his chair and cleared his throat. He started to speak once again, this time in a slightly more somber tone and slower, more calculated diction. He walked through the summary of Michael's three-week hospital history, starting with his primary injury known as an intraventricular hemorrhage or an aneurism which resulted in a substantial amount of bleeding in his brain. Dr. Wells described the surgical procedure he had performed in an attempt to relieve the pressure building up and compressing against Michael's brain tissue. Although they were able to create an outlet for the bleeding with some success, there was still significant swelling which had taken these number of weeks to resolve. Another pause and more shifting in chairs as the doctors took in some questions from family members. Most of the questions came from Michael's mom, who remained composed for the meeting though her cheeks were permanently blushed a red scarlet from all the evenings spent crying herself into a fitful sleep.

Kate stood against the wall throughout the conference as a silent observer. She had grown to love Michael's mother Helen who was a kind and caring soul and was at Michael's bedside often. Exhaustion had set in within the first week and continued to take its toll on Helen. Kate found herself taking care of two patients at times, making sure that Helen was eating and forcing her to go back to the hotel whenever rest was overdue. Kate tried to remain as hopeful as she could in her discussions with Helen while concurrently remaining true to the facts of Michael's condition and explaining it to Helen and the family as best as she could. The truth was Michael was not doing well at all.

Dr. Morris pulled up two M.R.I. brain scans on the screen of his laptop and turned it around for all to see. One image showed an M.R.I. of a normal and healthy brain. The one next to it was Michael's taken just the day before. The difference was obvious to all in the room. A large cavity had formed inside of Michael's brain. Dr. Morris explained how the location of the cavity where the initial bleed occurred had now resulted in the atrophy or the loss of brain tissue which formed the ominous void. It got worse. The location of this cavity was in the lower area of his brain which controlled critical functions like breathing and circulation.

Dr. Morris stopped once again to remove his glasses and rub his eyes. No one interrupted with questions. The doctor put his glasses back on and stared at the chart. He didn't need to. He knew what he was going to say next.

"Right now, the machines we have Michael on are keeping him alive. They're doing his breathing for him plus a various amount of other considerations. If the machines were to stop at this point, Michael would die."

Another pause to give time for his statements to land and clear the way safely for more to come. "Given these findings — Michael's unresponsiveness to stimulation of any kind, the M.R.I.'s and the location of the atrophy, at this time, we have little to no hope that Michael will ever recover enough to come off the machines currently keeping him alive," the doctor said as compassionately as he could.

The words sucked the air from the room and everyone held their breath as though trapped under water. Tears were forming in the eyes of Michael's sisters and mother. Kate touched a tissue to her eyes as well to keep them from spilling over. Her heart broke for this family that she had come to love. She also wrestled to reconcile the medical facts supporting each statement and the voice she now questioned if she had heard at all: "*My daughter. This man will make a full recovery.*" The words still churned inside of her like waves in a tempest mercilessly tossing a tiny boat wherever they wanted.

The doctor concluded his remarks with one last thought that still had to land in the room.

"We have the ability to keep Michael 'alive,' so to speak, for as long as we like. Of course the longer he remains on the machines the more likely there will be further complications. But the more important issue we have to consider at this point is quality of life. If we did keep Michael alive for, let's say years to come, is that the kind of existence Michael would want to have?" The question hung in the room until it could be absorbed by the collective imagination of everyone who heard it — imagery fit for nightmares.

"No one is under any pressure to answer this now," the doctor continued. "You are not being handed a time limit either. We will continue to give Michael and his whole family the best care we know how. But if you as a family come to the conclusion that this course of action is not what is best for Michael or yourselves, we are here to answer any other questions you might have on what the next steps would look like."

No one moved for a while. No further questions were asked. It was almost as though the silence summed it up and in the void of conversation everyone in the room had already answered the question for themselves. No one in that room wanted Michael to go on like that. It's not what he would want. Michael would soon be leaving them all for good. It was now just a matter of when.

Chapter 15: A Familiar Scene

The first thing I noticed was the banner above the trophy case. It read 'Home of the Marysville Grizzly Bears' and I was hit with a wave of nostalgia. The hallway I stood in was lined on both sides with familiar green lockers which were like streaks of color contrasted against the cream tones of the linoleum floor and painted white concrete ceiling. The smells and even the subtle resonance from the echo of someone walking on another floor at the far end of the hallway provoked memories from the many days I spent there as a young boy. I was standing in my old school.

Down the hall from where we stood and to the right was my old classroom. I recognized it by the art plastering the wall outside the door. Each student had traced an outline of their hand and drew art inside their hands and all around. A paper banner was taped above: 'What's Inside of Me?' Many of the students had drawn crosses and hearts. There were pictures of horses and ballet dancers, families standing together, and adventures the students had been on or wanted to experience. I found my hand print at the top far right. I wasn't standing close enough to make out the detail, but I could tell it was mine from memory. It was also the only one without any color because I had drawn simple bars covered with a smattering of musical notes. The music written inside my small hand print had actually been the first three bars to one of my first pieces. I remembered the teacher's look of dissatisfaction when I showed her. She said my art didn't "pop." I remembered the distain I harbored towards my classmates and teachers for their ignorance.

They have no idea, I had thought to myself.

But it became clear quickly that the Father had not brought me back here to revisit memories of my own. I realized that our focus was meant to be on someone else. Abruptly cutting through the quiet of the empty hallway, the frenzied wail of a familiar voice rang out: "No! You can't have that!"

That was my voice I thought to myself. Though I couldn't see inside I knew exactly what was happening and I shivered with a cold tremor, bracing myself for the remaining sounds to come. The shrill and agonizing cry from my cherished violin could be heard as it scratched out a piercing cacophony more offensive and tormenting than fingernails across a chalk board. I involuntarily found myself take a few steps forward as I thought to intervene, but the Father placed his arm across my path and stopped me from going any further. He didn't have to say anything. His eyes were like an ocean of compassion that swallowed up the trauma clutching at my soul. In one look I could see that he knew. He knew every ounce of anxiety, fear, and rage that was coursing through me in the moment as the little boy whose precious possession was being violated. He knew me as the nine-year-old and he knew me as the man. He knew me completely and yet his eyes brandished a fiery love that came without a hint of expectation or judgement.

I could hear my cries of protest coming from inside the classroom. Then I heard my violin shatter against the wall — my stomach twisted nauseous contortions. Yet my eyes remained fixed on the Father. The shriek flooding the hallway produced by my nine-year-old self sounded more like the moan from a soldier with a mortal wound writhing in the final throes of death. I saw in my periphery a teacher come running from another room down the hall towards the turbulent commotion. But I could no longer access the pain of the nine-year-old boy who I knew lay shattered in pieces on the floor with his violin. Staring into the Father's eyes while the sounds from my past violently roiled, they no longer crashed over me, pulling me down into despair. With him beside me, it was as though I now found myself standing upon the waves of childhood trauma, untouched by their churning hunger.

Travis Bishop emerged from the classroom in the clutches of a teacher marching him off towards a reckoning. I caught the look of fear in his eyes and the bruise discoloring the one on his left. I recalled the foreboding feeling of alarm which engaged my primal nine-year-old flight instincts when Travis filled the classroom doorframe on this day all these years ago. He was so intimidating and his bruised eye only added to the imposing aura. But now, as I watched this frightened boy get hauled away I recognized that the pain and fear from the moment in the sandbox for Travis continued to cast its shadow into the years of his youth as his childhood hell continued to rage inside his home.

As if in response to my thoughts, a vision opened in front of me like the illuminated projection on a screen. All my senses were immediately engaged in the scene unfolding before me. I saw Travis yelling as he ran towards his father looming ominously over his mom as she cowered in a corner with wide-eyed terror written on her face. "Leave her alone!" Travis yelled with a release of fury from the flames of his own internal inferno which had been smoldering for years. Travis didn't have time to react to what came next. I heard the clap of sound as the backhand from his dad came across his face in a rapid reflex like the recoil of a gun. I heard Travis's mom scream and watched the shock settle into Travis's widening eyes as he fell back to the floor.

"Don't you *ever* talk to me like that again you little shit or you'll get far worse!" his dad commanded with an imposing finger thrust towards Travis's face. The red imprint of his dad's hand was already starting to flare up before the vision was gone and I could see Travis and the teacher passing us in the hall.

As they walked by, Travis broke away from the teacher's grasp in a frenzied panic and raced towards the open door of the teacher's washroom. He slammed the door behind him and the lock on the handle clicked. The futile pounding and ultimatums from the teacher which followed were never acknowledged by Travis. From inside the washroom I could hear muffled sobs and pictured Travis quivering on the floor in the corner, unable to escape his situation — unable to escape the misery of life.

An hour would pass before two mothers arrived at the school because of a phone call they received regarding their children. Two nine-year-old boys lay unmoving and inconsolable inside the school on the floor, too absorbed in their own pain to be aware of the suffering felt by the other. They had both been victims. They had both suffered at the hands of another, but the only one who saw the story unfold that way in that moment was the Father — and now me. My childhood memory from the rest of this day had been lost in a fog. In fact, the weeks that followed this incident blurred and disappeared altogether as though hidden behind a dark grey cloud. I remained standing in the hallway with the Father, as now, a whole other side of the story began to play out before us.

Travis's mom arrived at the locked bathroom door and knelt down on the ground outside. She didn't knock, but placed a hand against the door and spoke in a gentle voice.

"Travis. Sweetheart. It's mom. I'm here. Do you want to come out and talk?" She asked, her words catching in her constricting throat.

"No," a subdued voice replied. I could still hear quiet sobs coming from the other side of the door. His mom didn't say anything back. She folded her hands in her lap and waited with the patient poise of one who had done this many times before. Minutes passed. The odd student would pass through the hallway and throw an awkward glance at the adult kneeling on the floor before walking on. Mom waited. Travis spoke again.

"Please don't tell Dad," he said in a quiet plea. Deep breaths mixed with more sniffling suggested that his crying had picked up again. "Please don't tell Dad." I could see that Mom had to think about her next words before talking to her son again.

"Honey, your dad never came back home after last night. I don't know where he's off to this time or how long he'll be gone, but I've been thinking about it and we're going to leave this time too. Just you and me." Mom paused to let her words settle before going on. "We're going to go live with Grandma for a while in Delaware. We haven't seen her for a long time and she would love to see you again." There was another silent pause for a while before the door handle made a click and creaked open with a crack large enough to reveal Travis's red eyes and tear-stained face.

"Hey pal," Mom said.

The door opened all the way and Travis threw himself around his mom's neck curling up in her lap as another dam broke, releasing more messy tears and sobs from a reservoir deep in his heart.

"I'm sorry. I'm sorry. I'm sorry. Please don't be mad at me, Mom. Please don't tell Dad. Please don't tell Dad." The remorseful refrain found its mark on his mom's heart and quickly pulled tears to the surface of her eyes as she hugged her son. "I didn't mean to do it, Mom. I'm so sorry. Please don't be mad with me Mom. Please don't be mad."

"It's okay, sweetheart. I know you are. I know you're sorry."

There was no lecture. By now even the teacher who had been standing at a distance had walked away to give the moment space and dignity. Travis remained in his mom's arms a while longer. I watched the two of them huddled together as they had been those years ago in a sandbox. Them against the world. A bell rang indicating the end of a class period and forced them to move and avoid the increased glances and crush from the swell of hallway traffic.

Two moms walked out of Marysville Elementary School that afternoon with their sons tucked under their arm like chicks under wing. The Father and I followed Travis and his mom out the front doors and into the parking lot. I never had a chance to look into my old classroom where I soaked the carpet with my tears, but as we walked out into daylight I caught a glimpse of my mom walking me out the back door to our car. She carried a garbage bag in one hand which I knew held the broken pieces of my violin. As I watched myself get into the car with my mom I remembered the pain which would fuel my hatred. I wished then that I had known this side of the story. From where the Father and I stood I could see both boys get into their cars, both of them damaged and bruised. Both of them loved deeply and seen by the Father. I hoped then that I could someday see Travis again.

Chapter 16: Alfie's Song

By the end of another long day on the street, Alfie had $87.28 resting at the bottom of his guitar case in an assortment of change and small bills. Alfie had staked his claim on the corner of Sixty-fifth and Columbus across from the Lincoln Centre for the past seven years. He had become a fixture on the side of the building which the locals had grown accustomed to seeing and hearing every day. Though his guitar had seen better days the sound of his music was pure and carried a substance to it that would often catch people passing by off guard. By his appearance, no one approaching him would expect to find themselves walking through a wave of sound that broke through all their senses penetrating to their heart and soul. A handful of unsuspecting pedestrians would stop and linger each day. Alfie would meet their eyes with a smile and continue his melody. Every so often a mist of moisture could be spotted in a stranger's eye which to Alfie, was worth more than a guitar case overflowing with cash.

It was on this familiar street corner where I would pass Alfie every morning and greet him, often dropping whatever spare change I had in his case. It was now on this street corner where the Father and I stood as Alfie was finishing his last song for the day. He still wore the same weathered Yankees ball cap, patterned sweater and blue windbreaker I had seen him in before. But his worn out attire remained a pale contrast to his vivacious smile and eyes that seemed to sparkle with the innocence of a playful child.

We stood only a few feet away as the sustain from his last chord faded into the bluster of a busy New York intersection. Alfie sat for a moment with a look of pleasure on his face, though there was no applause and no one on the street stopped to acknowledge his final tune. The peace enveloping him in that moment inferred he played for reasons of his own and an audience of One. And then, just as clearly as before, I saw the image of that horse once again pressing against the fence trying to taste the elusive fragrant flower.

"It's you," the Father said, looking at me.

"What's me?" I asked.

"The horse," he said. "You're the horse."

I shouldn't have felt surprised by this time at God Almighty knowing my every thought. Surely, I had been through enough to make this seem like a trifle. But I still felt myself recoil somewhat from the perceived intrusion before my curiosity brought about my next question.

"I don't understand what this vision means. If I'm the horse, what's with the flower?" Without hesitation the Father responded. "I delight deeply in this son of mine you see before you and he knows it. That is his peace and his joy — knowing my delight and favor that rests upon him so abundantly. This is the fragrance that you can perceive yet lack in your life though you possess every other good thing."

I returned a puzzled look to the Father. "I still don't understand though, what is it about this man's life that makes him feel you so deeply and play such a sweet sound when he sits here in rags and plays on an instrument that, by appearance, shouldn't even work?"

"Come and see," The Father said with a smile and started to follow behind Alfie, who by now, had returned his guitar to its case and started walking south.

After following Alfie a few blocks, he approached one of the old basilicas of New York with noble towers and beautiful stained glass which had overlooked the city since well before the turn of the 1900's. Alfie produced a key as he approached a side door and entered in. The entrance led to some stairs leading down into a hallway and opened up to multipurpose rooms where plastic tables and chairs had been set up in the open space. There was a large kitchen off to the side with a few people making soup and sandwiches around well-used preparation tables. Everything about the space was dated. The linoleum on the floors retreated to the edges of walkways where years of traffic had worn it down to concrete. The aqua green cabinets had rounded edges in places where they had once been square, exposing the smoothed plywood in places where they were handled regularly. The smell of the soup warming in an industrial-sized pot wafted through the corridors and clung to its low ceilings. To Alfie, this was the smell of home.

"Hi Alfie. Welcome back. Long day?" A man from inside the kitchen said as Alfie walked past the kitchen door.

"Yes Tom. Yes indeed. Another long day, that's for sure. Haha. Thank you, brother. Thank you."

Alfie continued past the kitchen and came to a door with a sign that said "Boiler Room" on it. Another key on his ring gained him access inside with a click. He switched on the lights; a few bare bulbs dangled freely by their wire from the ceiling. The light revealed the great industrial machines and maze of pipes which kept the church patrons warm in the cold winter months. Of course, when the church was first built, there was no central heating so the massive ducts and pipes which branched off in all directions had to be installed as an afterthought, and it showed.

Shelves with cleaning supplies neatly lined one corner of the

117

room. In another corner, tucked behind the boiler and pipes was a cot and a simple wooden stool doubling as a bedside table. On the table sat a simple bedside lamp, an old Bible, and a pair of reading glasses. Above the cot which had been neatly folded was a single five-by-seven photo which had been torn in one corner and taped to the concrete wall. Though the Technicolor print and the faded image of the picture displayed its age, the subjects were still discernible. A beautiful young black couple who looked to be in their late twenties beamed vibrant smiles into the camera as they held each other's hands while wrapping them together around the woman's swelling belly. The man in the picture flashed a resemblance to the one now resting his ratty guitar case against the wall, though they were now separated by many years. Alfie approached the photo on the wall and rested his hand right next to it as though tenderly brushing his hand through the elegant woman's hair.

"Mm boy, you sure do look fine this day, Mrs. Anderson. You're my beautiful garden rose. Mm-hm, yes you are." Alfie kissed the tip of his finger and pressed it against the photo and smiled.

"You girls take care now. I've got to be getting on again, but I'll be back soon. I love you."

Alfie returned to the door, shut the lights off, and closed it behind him. He approached the kitchen door again and this time walked in and greeted those inside. The man who had said hello to him earlier held up five individual bread bags with four sandwiches inside each bag.

Tom had been volunteering his time in the church's feeding and shelter program now for over twelve years since he retired from a long and successful career in law. He could have joined the rest of his colleagues who retired at the same time on a golf course or beach condo at any point along those years. But for six days a week, the homeless, marginalized, and poor of New York were his full-time job. He would have it no other way.

"Here you go, Alfie. Special order for the gentlemen," Tom said with a smile.

"Haha! Boy! Thank you, Tom. Thank you everyone. You all are just the sweetest bunch of angels God left down here," Alfie said.

"Well Alfie, we would have left years ago, but we can't go leaving our favorite angel behind now can we?" Tom said with a wink.

"Aw. You're all just too good. Just too good."

"Say hi to everyone for us, Alfie. God bless."

"Thank you. Thank you. God bless y'all."

Alfie retraced his steps now back up the stairs and out the side door of the church back onto the busy New York streets. Alfie was not a difficult quarry to track. His pace did not conform to the hurried bustle of the afternoon throng, racing along as though attempting to elude the regular rhythm of time. The Father and I ambled at a steady pace behind Alfie who walked along the sidewalk like it was a dirt road in the country.

His first stop was a busy grocery store a few blocks away. It was now the dinner hour and he converged into the narrow isles along with the rest of the city as they collected their dairy, produce, and meals for the evening. He walked up to the pharmacy counter and hit the little silver bell. A middle-aged woman in a white medical coat appeared from behind shelves of pills. I was immediately drawn to her eyes. They seemed to shine with a brilliant kindness, like lights reflecting across the water indicating safe harbor to ships wandering nearby in the night.

"Good evening, Alfie. You're here for Mrs. Jones's thyroid medication?" she said pleasantly.

"Hi Carla. Yes, that'd be about right." Alfie produced a paper from his pocket and unfolded it on the counter in front of Carla.

"The good doctor says this'll only be enough to get her through a week. Is that right?" Alfie asked, sounding concerned.

"Yes. It says here that Dr. Makenzie wants to see her again before prescribing any more. That shouldn't be a problem though, right?" Carla asked while studying the scribble on the prescription.

"Mm. Well, I sure hope not. You see, the thing of it is, elevator's broke in her place right now and she can't do those stairs too well. Let's just hope they get around to fixing it in time. I'm sure everything will be okay," Alfie said with as much confidence as he could find. But it was obvious that the situation didn't sit well with him as concern appeared across his face.

"I'll just be a few minutes with this Alfie," Carla said as she disappeared back behind his rows of shelves.

"Thank you, Carla. Thank you."

While he waited for the medication, he made good use of his time like an old pro who'd been up and down the aisles of the store hundreds of times before. A quart of milk and a dozen eggs from dairy. A box of crackers and a bag of granola. A loaf of bread, a box of tea, and a copy of the *New York Times*. Alfie returned to the counter a few minutes later with his items. Carla was waiting with the small bottle of pills. Now it was Carla with a look of concern on her face.

"Alfie, this medication still isn't covered by any plan, you know; and it's not cheap," she said as Alfie placed his goods down on the counter.

"Well, that's okay now. That's okay. How much is it?"

"One week's worth of medication comes to forty-two dollars," Carla said hesitantly.

"Have mercy. My, my. Yes, those are some pricey pills," Alfie replied while pulling out the money from his pocket he had collected from his guitar case earlier that day. "I hope this is going to be enough. I was also hoping to grab one of those nicotine gum packs, but let's see how we do first," he said counting out his money.

Carla rang in the medicine then scanned all his items on the counter.

"Looks like you'll be fine with this, but if we throw on the nicotine gum you'll be over by about twelve dollars," Carla said looking at the screen.

"That's alright, Carla. Yeah. That's alright. I'll be by tomorrow and see if I can't get it then," Alfie said, gracefully making the best of it.

Carla tilted her head, peered over her glasses, and looked Alfie over. Alfie returned an unsuspecting smile. There wasn't a hint of malice or disappointment in his humble demeanor. Carla knew Alfie would be back tomorrow and he'd produce more small bills to buy the nicotine gum and who knows what else that day. With a sigh and chuckle, Carla relented and reached behind her to grab the gum. She put the gum in the bag along with Alfie's other groceries and pulled out a twenty dollar bill from her purse from behind the counter before Alfie could raise a protest. She punched in the purchase and pulled out $7.20 change from the till and placed it on the counter before Alfie who returned a look of curious delight.

"Well now, Carla. What may I ask are you getting on about

here?" Alfie said, unable to hide his surprise.

"You take the gum and keep the change, Alfie. You can argue with me, but not until tomorrow when I see you back here again."

"My, my Carla. I sure am grateful for this. Thank you so much," Alfie said while shaking his head. "Thank you so much. God bless you."

"You take care of yourself, Alfie," Carla said with a grin of amusement as she turned to busy herself once again behind her shelves of bottles and pills.

The Father and I followed Alfie out of the store and back onto the streets where he continued at a purposeful but leisurely gait. Unlike so many bustling through the throngs of the city, I began to notice that Alfie was intentional about meeting people in the eye wherever he went and exchanged a graceful nod of affirmation. If you happened to be one of the lucky ones to catch his eye, you would remember it. A warm mixture of childlike delight and confident joy emanated from his glance, which would leave all those in his wake feeling as though they had just come face to face with a friend. We weaved our way through the congestive pother of New York, tracking behind Alfie as he passed through the crowd like a warm current cutting through a cold ocean.

The walk stretched on block after block before Alfie turned in towards a large housing complex. The complex was comprised of rows and columns of aged brick apartments that had once been considered high during their time but had since become dwarfed by the sprawling metropolis and towers that now broke into the vault of hazy sky. Alfie wandered through the uniform rows until turning in and stopping at apartment tower 3B. It looked no different than all the others: tired red brick façade accented with spires of black iron stairs clinging to its sides like wisteria on a trellis. He approached the doors to the entrance and pressed the red button next to the faded numbers 425 – Jones. A voice through a static line crackled to life from the receiving end of the speaker.

"Hello?"

"Evening Gloria. It's Alfie. How are you today?" Alfie spoke close to the receiver in the wall. The sound of excited young children's voices could be heard breaking through the static in the background in response to his voice.

"Shh. Hush now," the voice said, speaking away from the microphone. And then, "Come on up Alfred," before another buzz indicated that Alfie could open and walk through the entrance door. The added weight from the steel-reinforced mesh on the door caused it to close with a slam that echoed down the concrete corridor hallway. Taped up on the wall next to the bank of mailboxes was a note with the words: ELEVATOR OUT OF ORDER. PLEASE USE STAIRS. – MANAGEMENT.

That notice had been posted now for two months. Derogatory graffiti on the paper and the wall around it gave voice to the growing frustration felt by the tenants in this longstanding inconvenience. Alfie studied the note and wondered to himself if it would still be up a week from now — when Gloria would have to get to the doctor.

"Lord have mercy," he whispered to himself as he shook his head and walked down the main hallway. The incandescent light was inconsistent, interrupted with patches of shadow where bulbs had burned out and were never replaced. A cold institutional glare flickered from the remaining light bulbs encaged in wire frames. There was a stench of urine and cigarette smoke lingering in the stale air of the corridor because the ventilation system was not capable of providing an adequate flow of fresh air to the building—

and that was when it was working.

The first door Alfie came to was on the main floor. He knocked lightly at door number 111 and leaned in close to speak.

"Evening Dennis. It's Alfie. I've got some sandwiches here for you," he announced and waited patiently for a response.

There was a commotion coming from within and then a brawling voice detonated from behind the door. "I don't need no fucking charity from the likes of you or your kind! Fuck off before I come out there and mess you up!" The voice bellowed in a rage. As irrational as I knew my fear was, I found myself inadvertently take a few steps back at the sound of the threatening voice. Alfie just smiled to himself as he placed the bag of sandwiches down at the threshold. He stood upright again and lingered for a few reflective moments with his eyes closed. In the silence I knew the Father could hear every word as Alfie brought Dennis before him in a silent prayer. With a nod of his head which I could tell indicated 'Amen' Alfie opened his eyes and continued on down the hall towards a stairway and the Father and I followed.

Alfie climbed one flight and stepped out into another hallway on the first floor going now to door 214. Another knock and announcement.

"Evening Walt. It's Alfie. You home?" Alfie inquired.

I heard odd footsteps approaching the door: shuffle—clump—shuffle—clump. It took a bit longer than expected, but eventually the door opened to reveal a white-haired man in a plaid housecoat and a cast on his left leg, leaning on some crutches. He beamed a big smile which produced more wrinkles along his lined face and exposed what few teeth remained in his mouth.

"Alfie! It's good to see you, my friend. How are you?" Walt

offered with a warm greeting.

"Doing just fine, Walt. Just fine indeed. How's that leg of yours holding up now? I see they haven't gotten around to fixing that elevator just yet."

"Bagh, don't get me started on that." Walt dismissed with a wave of his hand. "Do you want to come in and stay for a while?"

"Well that's awful kind of you Walt, but I best be getting on. Just a few more folks I need to see yet. But thank you." Alfie sorted through some of his bags and found the *New York Times*. He held that out to Walt with a bag of sandwiches. "Here, Walt. Thought you might want to catch up on how your team's been doing. Bit of supper for you too."

Walt reached for the gifts and received them with a smile. "Thank you, my friend. God bless you."

"God bless you too, Walt. You take care of that leg now. I'll come by for that visit real soon," Alfie said as he gathered his bags again and started back down the hallway. After one more flight of stairs and another hallway, Alfie stood outside of door 324. He knocked and offered his greeting once again to whoever was inside.

"Evening Beverly. It's Alfie. How you doing?"

Footsteps rumbled the floor as the resident inside approached. The door opened issuing a wafting smell of cigarette smoke into the hallway as Beverly stepped through the door and immediately absorbed Alfie into a big bear hug.

"How you doing Alfie! It's good to see you here." Everything about Beverly was boisterous and extra-large from her personality to her clothing size. She appeared to be in her mid-thirties and had lived on her own for a while, though from time to time a different gentleman companion would appear in the background whenever

125

Alfie made an appearance. She was warm and welcoming when her friend came to see her at the door and appeared to be alone this time.

Alfie reached down for a bag holding the sandwiches and the nicotine gum and handed it to her. "It's wonderful to see you to, my child. You're looking mighty pretty this evening. Mighty pretty indeed. I brought you a few things. Thought you might appreciate some fine home cooking," Alfie said with a playful chuckle and a gleam of affection in his eye. Beverly opened the grocery bag and looked up at Alfie with a smile.

"Thank you, friend. How did you know I had a hankering for ham and cheese?"

"I just don't want to see a beautiful girl like yourself wasting away. You keeping well these days?"

"Mm-hm," she replied, but stared down at the floor as if to say things could be better. After a moment where neither of them moved, she looked up to meet Alfie's eye again. They were unlike any other eyes she had ever looked into. While every other pair of eyes Beverley had ever surveyed in her life either judged or wanted something from her, she found in Alfie's gaze only love and compassion. Just a look from him could make her tear up—he was the only man in her life who ever made her feel cherished like a daughter. He was the only person who truly saw her.

"You know I'm still going to quit one of these days soon," she said. Her words lacked the confidence she hadn't been able to carry for herself in the long four years she'd been trying to quit.

Alfie looked at her and loved her. "I know you will, child. I know you will. You're a beautiful shining star in this world and they can't ever get to your light on the inside. You can do anything.

Anything! You're loved by God Almighty and ain't nobody that can say otherwise." He placed his hand on her shoulder as he spoke, hoping the physical connection would help his words connect with her heart. She embraced him again in her doorway as tears brimmed in her eyes.

"Thank you," she said in a whisper as her closed eyes forced a tear to roll down her cheek. Alfie leaned in and embraced her with an affectionate hug.

"I love you, Beverly. You're never alone, girl. You hear? You're never alone. You've got the Father right there with you always and he loves you more than this very life itself." Alfie said in a muffle as they remained in their embrace.

I could feel delight emanate off the Father like heat thrown from the sun as we stood in the hall together watching this display of kindness and affection. We stood as silent witnesses to this special moment that captured the attention of the Almighty and touched him deeper than a thousand songs of praise ever could. Alfie said goodbye to his friend with a few more kind words and continued on to more stairs.

When Alfie stopped in front of door 425, he paused to catch his breath before knocking. He had travelled far after an already long day and weariness was slowly starting to settle in — but only the Father and I saw it. The door opened without a knock from Alfie and he picked himself up tall and straight and wore the same smile he'd been using all day. As the door opened, three children burst out as though they had been standing on a coiled spring. Alfie had to hold his hands up in the air and protect the groceries from getting caught in the crush from the children who clung to his side. The hall was filled with everyone's laughter including Alfie's.

"Haha! There's my angels! There they are. You kids are going to knock poor Alfie right down off his feet one of these days. You know that? Hahaha!" The celebration in the hallway was interrupted by another voice from inside the apartment.

"Tyrell! Oscar! Talliah! You guys keep all that hoopla up there's going to be everyone yelling in this hall before we know it." The woman remained deep inside the apartment as she shouted her reprimand. "C'mon now. Get inside"

"You kids listen to your grandma and let poor old Alfie come inside too," Alfie added. The children released him from their grip and ran back inside, leaving Alfie once again standing at the doorway catching his breath. He stepped across the threshold and closed the door behind him. The Father and I followed and passed through the closed door as though it didn't exist, and we were all standing inside apartment 425.

Everyone was down the hall waiting for Alfie inside the living room. He tucked into the small kitchen first and placed his bags on the side table which could barely fit inside the tiny space. He placed the sandwiches, milk, and eggs inside the fridge and put all the remaining groceries away in the cupboard. He reached inside his pocket and pulled out the five and two single dollar bills which Carla had given him. It was placed inside a plain paper envelope on the counter which had 'Rent' written on it. Grabbing the small pill jar he acquired at the pharmacy, he opened it and placed one gently in his palm. He poured water in a small glass and walked into the living room where everyone was waiting.

"Hello Gloria," he said with an affectionate smile and approached a woman sitting in her wheelchair in the corner of the room. Gloria looked to be about the same age as Alfie—which I guessed at about sixty something. She was a knitter and one of her latest creations lay sprawled across her lap while the two needles lay dormant on a side table next to her, still clinging to loose threads that trailed off into the ongoing weave. Her dark brown skin had a healthy complexion, but sagged under her neck and below her arms. She wore a simple blue housecoat over a white undershirt and a loose-fitting light pair of grey sweatpants which stopped well above her ankles and drew more attention to the bright pink slippers she wore on her bare feet.

Gloria had a warm smile waiting for Alfie as she returned the greeting. "Hello Alfie. It's good to see you."

Alfie placed her pill and glass of water on the side table next to her. "We're going to have to pray about that elevator, kids. It's hard enough for your grandma to get around even when it's working." Alfie collapsed on the couch where the kids waited patiently for him to sit before they could assault him with affection once again. It had been all day since Alfie had actually sat in a chair let alone something as comfortable as an old couch. If left undisturbed he would have certainly been asleep within a quick minute, but in the next second, a small boy who looked to be the youngest of the three children, no older than six, crawled onto his knee. Sleep would have to wait.

"Hello there, Tyrell. How are you doing, champ?" The other two kids, an older brother who I assumed was Oscar and looked to be about ten years old, and a sister who must have been Talliah and looked to be about twelve, snuggled into Alfie on either side of him.

"Alfie, do you know what? I jumped over a fire hydrant today." The words burst out of Tyrrell's mouth in proud proclamation.

"You did not, Tyrell! You jumped beside it and it wouldn't have been high enough!" the older boy objected.

"Leave him be, Oscar," Talliah intervened. "You probably can't jump over one either."

"Hush now every one of you. Lord have mercy. Let's not get to arguing before poor Alfie even has a chance to catch his breath," Gloria chided.

But Alfie just chuckled with his same joyous vitality, welcoming the interaction with an attentive smile on the kids.

"Oh, it's okay, Gloria. I don't mind. These kids have more energy to spare than you and me combined."

"Ha! Don't I know that!" Gloria chortled.

"Besides," Alfie continued, addressing the children now, "I bet each one of you could jump over the moon with those fancy new shoes of yours. You remember when I saw you kids for the first time? Y'all weren't even wearing shoes."

Alfie studied their shoes and remembered back to the day he saw the three scraggly looking kids show up to Mass at his church one Sunday morning those few months ago. They had sat at the back close to where Alfie often sat. Right away Alfie had noticed them. Their clothes had been dirty and torn and the boys had no shoes on their feet while Talliah's runners were coming loose at the soles.

Curiosity and compassion drew him to the children and he intercepted them at the end of the service before they could run off. They had just recently come to live with their grandma Alfie learned, as he started to talk with the three. Their mom had been taken away again, this time probably for longer. Their grandmother had told them to get to church that morning so they'd walked a few blocks until they came to the first one they found; it was Alfie's.

Alfie walked them home that day and befriended Gloria along with her three grandchildren. Gloria was barely getting by herself, bound to a wheelchair and stuck on the fourth floor. Her daughter was in jail, and now with the elevator broken, so was Gloria. It took a few weeks, but Gloria and the kids were immediately added to Alfie's daily visitation roster and soon he started stopping by with food and new clothes from the donation centers in town. But Alfie bought their new shoes at a store. Each pair cost the equivalent of a full day's guitar case in earnings, but seeing the children's joy made the purchases worth every single penny.

Alfie sat in silence on the couch reminiscing and yielding to a much needed moment of rest while the kids continued to bicker and spar on Alfie's lap.

"Hush now. Hush," Alfie said calmly with his hands raised in the air. That was all it took to regain the order of the room.

For a few hours, the five of them were family as they sat in the living room talking, laughing, and telling stories. There was a small stack of books which Alfie had brought with him one day from the library, which he read through while the children listened and forgot their anxieties for a few wonderful moments. Gloria wished she could do the same and forget her troubles. But there was so much worry waiting in her future and so much pain still revisiting her from the past. Her own well-being was important once again, if only for her grandchildren. What if something happened to her? What was going to happen to them? It wasn't a friendly world they were growing up in, which Gloria and her daughter had already come to learn.

They read through the stack of library books while eating the sandwiches Alfie had brought. When they were done reading and had eaten dinner it was time for the couch to pull out into a bed for the three children. Alfie set it up while the kids each took their turn in the single washroom of the apartment. When they were all settled in, Alfie sat at the foot of the bed and said a simple prayer of thanks and blessing over Gloria and her grandchildren. He kissed each one on the forehead and said goodnight. At the door he leaned over and embraced Gloria in a hug.

"You take care now. I'll be back tomorrow and we'll see if we can't figure something for those pills of yours," Alfie said.

"Thank you Alfie," Gloria said. She'd been fighting back tears all evening but couldn't hold them back any longer as they now started to flow in their embrace. "God bless you. God bless you."

"Good night, Alfie," the kids said from their bed as Alfie turned back to the doorway.

Alfie reached to open the front door and stepped back into the hall. "God bless you, Gloria."

The Father and I retraced our steps behind Alfie as we wound back down the stairs to the ground floor. As we walked past Dennis's apartment, I noticed that the bag of sandwiches Alfie had left were now gone. Alfie noticed too and smiled.

Back outside the apartment the sun had retreated behind the horizon in the west, leaving the city towers to blend in with the dusk of the sky and cast their shadows far into the Atlantic Ocean. Alfie was navigating his regular return route when a commotion coming from a back alley drew his attention as he crossed its dark open mouth. Just a few feet in from the sidewalk a man was doubled over and vomiting violently onto the pavement. Though Alfie's tired feet must have urged him to continue forward, he stopped and regarded the man with a look of recognition—he had seen him somewhere before.

"Damien? That you?" Alfie asked as he stepped into the alley shadow.

The man continued to spew bile, gasping and groaning in between convulsions. All Alfie could make out was incoherent rambling as he got down on one knee beside him.

"Damien, it's me Alfie, from the church. I've sat with you in our kitchen a few times before, remember?"

Damien could only groan a response. He wore a black leather jacket and what little skin was left exposed had been covered in tattoos. One on his neck read D.N.R. A string of mucus and vomit dangled from Damien's nose and mouth and mixed with the discarded waste commonly scattered across the forgotten alleys of New York. The smell was repugnant. Alfie stayed beside him rubbing Damien's back while the episode ran its course.

"It's okay, my friend. I'm right here with you. You're going to be just fine," Alfie said in a calm voice.

This went on for some time before Damien's incoherent mumbles collected into the first sentence Alfie could understand. His words came out in a panicked scream.

"Don't touch my stuff, man! Hey! Don't touch my stuff!" Damien stammered in a delirious slur, presumably the effects of some form of some drug-induced psychosis.

"C'mon now. Let's get you home with me," Alfie said.

Alfie struggled to get Damien's half-dead weight vertical, and strained as he lifted him to his feet, clutching his one arm over his shoulder. With his other free hand, Alfie pulled a handkerchief from his pocket and wiped the mucus and residue that still mired and hung loosely from Damien's face. Damien continued to mumble and groan incoherently as they made their way back towards the sidewalk drawing stares from the crowds who gave them a wide birth as if they were sharks swimming through a school of fish. It was only a few more blocks to the church, but Alfie's stride was substantially slowed under the added weight of Damien shuffling along beside him. Tom was just locking up the front door of the church when he spotted Alfie come around the corner laden with his extra burden.

"Oh no. I'm sorry Alfie, but all the beds are taken tonight. We can't take any more," Tom said as he met Alfie at the bottom of the cascading front entrance stairs.

"That's okay Tom" Alfie said as he trudged by. "That's okay. He's with me tonight."

Alfie turned the corner and headed towards the side door, leaving Tom standing at the stairs shaking his head with an unbelieving grin before chasing after his friend to help.

"You just don't stop, do you Alfie?" Tom said as he lifted Damien's other arm over his shoulder and helped Alfie get him inside the building and down the stairs, the Father and I following close behind.

They arrived in the boiler room and sat Damien down on Alfie's bed before laying him across the neatly folded covers.

"I'll see if I can find you another mattress from upstairs and bring down some more sheets and pillows," Tom said, heading back towards the boiler room door.

"Thank you, Tom. God bless you," Alfie said, breathing a sigh of relief to once again be resting his feet as he sat on the far corner of his bed. He didn't stay in that position for long before he was back on his feet removing Damien's shoes and placing them neatly at the foot of the bed. Damien was snoring loudly and didn't stir as Alfie wrestled to get him under the bedcovers he had been lying on top of. Satisfied that his guest would be comfortable, Alfie returned his gaze to the picture taped to the wall.

"Evening Mrs. Anderson. Looks like we're not alone tonight," Alfie said, letting out a gracious chuckle. He then set his eyes back on Damien and placed a hand on his shoulder and spoke to God as though he was in the room right beside him. "They just don't know how loved they are, do they?"

Then I heard the Father speak a response as he stood beside me. "No. They do not."

Alfie stayed with his hand on Damien for a few moments before Tom returned. "This old mattress is all I could find. It's kind of thin but it's better than the floor. I grabbed a few extra blankets that might be able to go under it," Tom said, placing the mattress, blankets, and pillow on a space on the floor. He did his best to make it all as comfortable and inviting as he could.

"Thank you, Tom. That's mighty kind of you," Alfie said, still facing Damien with his hand on his shoulder.

"Wish there was more I could do tonight. I'm going to go out and get some new mattresses tomorrow so we don't keep getting stuck like this. Maybe I'll buy you a bunk bed," Tom said with a laugh.

"I sure am grateful, Tom. You can be sure of that." Alfie hung his jacket on a hook on the wall and changed into a clean shirt—one that didn't smell like vomit.

"I'll see you tomorrow. Good night." Tom returned back into the hallway leaving Alfie alone with Damien—and us.

"Good night, Tom."

Alfie did not get ready for sleep, to my surprise. Instead, he went to the corner of the room and picked up a mop and bucket full of cleaning supplies and walked back into the hallway. The Father

135

and I followed as he began to work his way throughout the church.

He hummed "Amazing Grace" while he travelled both floors and cleaned its six bathrooms. He finished off in a side room with a shower in the corner which had been added as an afterthought. He would not shower himself until later the next morning; he was too tired to go through with it tonight. He returned to his room thirty minutes later to replace the cleaning supplies and was happy to see Damien still sleeping soundly. He was safe. He felt glad that he could do this for his friend who he knew would encounter a rough awakening wearing a heavy burden of shame. Alfie would be there to talk with him and help lift it back off.

One more time Alfie left his room and walked upstairs; this time he entered the sanctuary. He settled into a middle row of pews and knelt down on the padded kneeling bench attached to the pew in front of him and began to pray. It was probably the first time Alfie had experienced silence in his entire day. For the whole afternoon, I had followed this man around with the Father and observed all that he packed into it. Though I could not feel the effects of fatigue myself, I admired the endurance with which he carried himself throughout the day for the sole benefit of others.

The Father and I remained at the back of the sanctuary. I watched while the Father listened. While we attended in reverent wonder, I saw the natural light from the moon blur with the city's incandescence as it travelled through the vaulted stained glass windows towering over the sanctuary. It cast a luminosity of pigments high into the vaulted ceiling above and across the decorative sacraments below like a mist of jewels.

For twenty minutes Alfie's silent prayer filled the sanctuary like a plume of aromatic incense and I recalled once again the vision I had of the flower with the fragrance pulling me into its alluring mystery. Here was a man whose battered songs dissolved often unnoticed into the turbulent din of busy New York City streets every day, yet his music pulled on the very fabric of heaven captivating the heart of God Almighty like a child pulling on his father's shirt.

As Alfie knelt silently in the pew with his head bowed I could sense the connection he made to the Father and the Father to him. This man had built a highway to the throne of God by living his life like this every day. I stood there watching him traverse unobstructed on its wide expanse and felt a longing rising up inside of me. One that had been there some distant time ago, but had faded altogether when I began to sink deep into the swells of life.

A flood of euphoric recall surged inside and I remembered the time I first awakened to my love for music. I couldn't just hear the inflections of melodious refrain as a young child. I could hear heaven itself which pulled at my heart like the yearning for home calling to a weary traveler's soul. I had forgotten, but Alfie helped me to see what had been missing for a long time. Now revisiting in my mind all the occasions I had dropped my meager pocket change in his open guitar case I wanted more than ever to have the chance to return one day and fill it with every hope and dream Alfie had ever desired.

His time of reflection and prayer coming to a close, Alfie rose from his spot, crossed himself and stepped back into the main aisle of the sanctuary. As he walked towards the doors at the back, he reached into his pocket and pulled out a quarter, a nickel, and a dime, his last forty cents from the day. Reaching the back doors where we stood off to the side, he let the coins drop from his hands into the small wooden alms box fastened to the wall. The sound of the coins inside the hollow wood coffer resonated against every wall and vaulted ceiling in the sanctuary, like a crescendo in a great musical masterpiece that commanded an audience to their feet in elevated applause. But there was no fanfare and no great audience to witness this man's life, except for the Father and I who now watched him returning to his room. Here he would sleep on a cold floor, while a stranger slept off the effects of a binge in his bed.

The Father turned and spoke to me once again: "We're returning to the meadow. There is more to see which will set your heart at rest."

Chapter 17: Precious Hours

Helen Mann lay on the hospital bed next to her son. Under normal circumstances, the white rhythmic noise from the breathing machines would put most people to sleep. But sleep eluded Helen for most of the evening. She did not want to allow sleep to steal away any more precious hours that she could spend physically at her son's side. It would not be long now before what remained of Michael would disappear for good, leaving only memories to hold on to. In less than twenty-four hours, they would turn the machines off which had kept him alive since he arrived at the Mt. Zion I.C.U.

Kate Wylder had already worked her shift for the day and spent an additional hour sitting with Helen and Michael's three sisters in his room around the bed. Over the course of a month, her compassion and care for Michael and his family had earned her a spot in their hearts. The hours around Michael's bed had been filled with laughter as Helen, Faith, Felicity, and Madeline regaled Kate with some of their favorite memories from their childhood together.

Like the time Michael had asked all his sisters for a concert audience in the living room when he was seven. The girls did not disappoint and gathered every stuffed animal they could find and packed the living room for a sold-out show. When the sisters were all in their teens and boys became more a part of their lives, Michael would have a way of letting his sisters know if he liked a particular boy by coming around the side of the house at night when his sister was being dropped off from a date and serenading them with his violin.

"Yup, it's funny—Michael never serenaded me when Brad and I were dating," Felicity said and the room erupted with a knowing laughter.

"Oh, I forgot about him. He was like your worst boyfriend ever!" Faith added before the laughter could subside.

Around eight-thirty Jessie arrived and the laughter stopped. Though countless times over the course of Michael's hospitalization the family tried to offer Jessie support and comfort, she remained cold and withdrawn not wanting to spend time even with her own mother when she arrived from out of town. Kate said goodnight to everyone and the sisters all returned to their places for the evening. Helen stepped out into the waiting room of the I.C.U. while Jessie had a visit alone with Michael. Jessie's visits usually didn't last long.

Jessie came back out into the waiting room around 10 p.m. and tapped Helen on the shoulder. Jessie's face was still red where the tears streaked her face in lines.

"You can go back in with him," Jessie said solemnly, while she stared blankly into the distance, her thoughts and emotions obviously carrying her somewhere far away where no one else was welcome.

"How are you doing, Jessie?" Helen had asked that question a thousand times out of sincere concern with the same response every time.

"I'm fine," Jessie would always say before returning behind the well-established fortifications of her heart protecting her from everyone who tried to get near.

Jessie's conflicted inner turmoil was exposed when her eyes unintentionally met with Helen's. For a fleeting moment, a connection appeared between them like warm breath on a cold window. They stood together on fragile common ground in their sense of loss and love they shared over Michael. Jessie had not even been sure herself if she ever really loved him. How could she love someone while being so unfaithful? How could she feel love for anyone else when she had none even for herself? But the love she found in Helen's eyes—both for Michael and for her—surprised her. It betrayed the emotions she had worked so hard at denying within herself. And then, the moment was gone.

"I'm fine," she replied with a lack of conviction.

She turned and walked out of the waiting room before further unveiled emotion could discredit her words. As she left the hospital she looked up at the sky as she walked to her car in the lot. It was clouded over, which seemed fitting for her thoughts. She felt alone. She hated herself for who she was and what she was doing. She couldn't reconcile the mix of sorrow, guilt and relief she was facing at the loss of her husband and felt like there wasn't a soul in the world she could talk it through with. Especially God.

The clouds blocking out the heavens only served to feed her feeling of loneliness. "Like you care anyways!" She spat out under her breath as she stared up at the blanketed night sky giving voice to her bitterness and pain. Michael would be gone tomorrow and a new chapter of her life could begin. Though the closer Jessie got to the turn of the page she realized there was likely to be no happy ending at the end of her story. She would remain trapped in her isolation and shame with no hope of rescue.

***

Inside the hospital, Helen returned to her son's room and closed the door behind her. No nurse would disturb her. They all knew what lay ahead and now only had to maintain the machines and their patient's comfort for a little while longer, which did not take up much of their time. Helen climbed onto her son's bed and lay on a spare pillow next to him. It wasn't long after her head touched the pillow that she began to cry a steady current of tears. What was life doing? It seemed like such a short time ago she lay in a hospital bed holding her sleeping child in her arms, welcoming him into the world with a gentle lullaby. Now, in another hospital bed at the other end of the country she lay next to her sleeping child still unable to accept the fact that it would be her last time to look upon his beautiful face. Everything for Helen as a mother up until this point had come so naturally as she cared for, raised, and admired her children while they grew. But no mother was meant to watch her child slip from life to death. Her heart told her so as it broke in a thousand different ways. A mother's heart was not made for this.

By 5 a.m., Helen was ready to return to the hotel room and hopefully escape her sorrow while her body rested for a few hours. She planned to be back at the hospital by noon. They had set the time to turn the machines off for 3 p.m. Madeline was there at five to stay by Michael's bed and make sure her mom went home to rest. Both of them had red around their eyes from the abiding presence of grief. There didn't seem a way to turn off the tears these days, as the internal gear that regulated their flow was breaking along with their hearts. Kate's shift would start at seven and she would join the rest of the family that day in soaking the ground with sorrow. After that, no one knew. Today would be a day they would all have to endure together. Not even the next sunrise after that was a promise that any of them could rely on.

Chapter 18: Alfie's Tree

The Father and I still stood in the church sanctuary where Alfie had just finished praying. Alfie's coins dropping in the alms box resonated across the great vaulted ceilings of the space. But instead of fading back into silence, an ascension of sound began to slowly build in volume and musical quality. It sounded like the rushing roar of a thousand waterfalls ascending with an orchestra and a choir all at once in a beautiful accompaniment of music I had never heard before. The sound grew more intense as though I were somehow falling towards it at a great speed. A light appeared, subtle at first, as a star surrounded by the dark of night, but it grew with the music until I was enveloped once again in its radiance.

Once again there was a soft overlay of meadow grass under my feet where I stood in place of the sanctuary floor. I knew the Father was still standing with me. I could feel him close, but the first thing I noticed was the tree. I stood on top of a hill overlooking a great forest of tall trees which spread off in all directions in the distance; but one tree held my complete attention. It was impossible to miss. Imagine the tallest tree you've ever seen stretching high towards the firmament. At its base it would take a number of grown men locking their hands together to make a circle around the circumference of its trunk. But the tallest trees of our world and imagination would only just touch the underside of the first branch of the tree I now beheld. This great tree was taller than the largest building in New York!

I surveyed the rest of the forest growing beneath its vast canopy;

there was no other tree like it anywhere else within sight. My gaze became fixed at its roots as I began to realize a distinct feature it possessed, unlike all the other trees of the forest. Besides the fact that the base of the great tree was as broad as a city block, at its foundation was a massive stump. The stump itself was alive and it fed the great tree like oxygen feeds a flame. I wasn't sure how I perceived this, but how else could a tree grow to this size unless it was connected to an abundant life giving supply? Large roots as thick as a locomotives clung to the stump on all sides, like a starfish fastened to a large rock, before diving deep into the forest floor below. To support the colossal tree, the stump had grown in size proportionately and was as large as a college stadium.

Growing throughout its thick canopy of leaves was what appeared to be clusters of fruit with the appearance of figs. They were small in proportion to the tree, but all the same, one fig could feed a brigade of men. The figs grew in abundance and even from our distant vantage, I could smell their intermingled aroma of sweet and spice.

The surrounding forest was not thick. Every individual tree grew spaced apart from another and lush green grass carpeted the forest floor. There was not one fallen dead branch or leaf to be seen. There was no sign of death anywhere at all. Besides the trees, flowers of all kinds burst out of the ground in an array of dazzling color and luminescence. There was light everywhere! Every living plant and creature gave off a light of its own, which only added to the surrounding brilliance. Though the great tree and the forest below stretched out far and wide, there was no hint of a shadow to be seen.

The music that brought me to this place continued until it was a symphony all around. Every birdsong along with the slightest breeze came together in a beautiful harmony complimenting the melodies surrounding me. The music came from everywhere as far as I could tell, but its essence originated from the tree.

There were people everywhere. But two individuals caught my attention as it seemed as though I had seen them somewhere before. It occurred to me then that I could make out features in great detail despite the distance from where we stood. A gorgeous woman with resplendent ebony skin sat at the base of the great tree leaning against one of the mighty roots. Her beauty was breathtaking and like everything else, she was emanating a light of her own that shone through her very complexion like luminous refractions on a polished black gem.

In front of her sat a young girl who looked to be no older than six or seven. I knew they were mother and daughter. The mother was weaving intricate braids with beads of brilliant color and precious materials in her daughter's hair. And she was singing. Hers was a song all of its own while accompanying the great tree's song in a fascinating harmony I never thought possible within the confines of musicality. Woven throughout the refrain of her aria, themes of gratitude and joy flowed like a substance as tangible as a touch. Her song was made much more profound as it blended with a deep sorrow painfully known in another life and another world. It made this woman's song the most beautiful thing I had ever heard so far.

"My son." The Father spoke to me though neither of us took our gaze off of the tree and the pair sitting beneath its sanctuary of branches and leaves. "Do you know where we are?"

I could have guessed heaven, but the word itself now seemed to fall short knowing now what I had come to experience and learn. Within the realms of eternity was an infinite expanse of worlds and places still beyond comprehension and measure. He was constantly creating, always singing, and new life would always follow.

"I don't," I said, feeling satisfied with my answer.

Expecting such a response, the Father went on: "This great tree was once just a small seed. I planted it myself inside the stump when the one you call 'Alfie' left this place and was born into the world."

At that statement my mind spun with a snarl of questions all vying for my voice at once. I remembered the first meadow where I stood while the Father sang a song over the little girl. The stump had been no larger than a small coffee table then. How had this one come to be so enormous? Who were all the others gathered in this place beneath the great tree? And the mother and daughter... where had I seen...?

I stopped mid-thought as the image of the old tattered photo taped to the wall in Alfie's makeshift bedroom flashed across my mind. The beautiful woman under the tree held a resemblance to the pregnant woman in the photo and the little girl must have been... This was Alfie's family—his wife and daughter! The profound revelation did nothing to calm the questions in my mind still trying to find my voice. But nothing came. The Father continued with his response.

"This stump was once small like the one you saw earlier when the little girl was sent from this place. It was small the day I planted Alfie's seed as well—but its roots are deep and living. As Alfie's tree grew from a sapling to the great tree it is now, the stump has grown with it. No one's tree can grow independent of the deep roots, nor can a tree grow larger unless the stump grows with it, lest it becomes weak under its own strength and falls. This tree has become great because its connection to the stump is deeply rooted.

Not only has life been drawn up as it grew, every infection and infirmity has been drawn down, having been absorbed into its living foundation."

I was thrown by the last statement. It seemed the more I learned here, the less I felt I knew. There was one question which now made its way to the top after hearing more about the stump: infection and disease? Where exactly were we? Hesitantly I asked, "Father, are we in heaven?"

"We are in one of the many places you would call by that name. Yes."

"Then how could a tree that grows here have an infection or infirmity? I thought that no sickness or disease grew in heaven." I felt confident my statement could be backed up by what I had learned in Sunday School.

The Father returned a look of amusement, free of judgement or distain, and answered: "Every tree growing on a stump here represents a life in the world. They grow in this place as they grow in their connection to me. The rest of the trees in the meadow which grow out of the ground grow and reproduce as they were created to do. They can only echo and accompany the songs being sung all around them. But every tree growing in the deep roots of the stump has been given a song which is theirs alone to sing." At this he hesitated. A look of sorrow appeared on his face. It was the closest thing to a shadow I had seen in the meadow so far.

He continued, slower than before, looking off into the distance. "Many have lost the sound of their own song and have forgotten where they come from. Their trees, even though they grow here, become sick and weak. Instead of filling the world with the song I sang over them—which is embodied with love, grace, and peace— they embrace fear, doubt, and pain because they have lost connection with their roots. With me."

I nodded in silence as I seemed to understand a little of what he was saying. He continued.

"But the one you call Alfie knows me. And his song is still a vibrant melody in your world. My heart beats within his and his in mine. All those you see who have come to gather around his tree are those who have left the world and are drawn here by his familiar tune. While they were in the world, they encountered its melody when this man showed them my love. They each have trees growing here of their own, but they gather here to celebrate in a community — brought together through this man's love and mine. They were the forgotten, the marginalized, and the poor. The one you call Alfie reminded them who they were — sons and daughters of great worth, and of their place here in me."

The Father's voice went silent and we stood for a time awash in the splendor of the beauty all around. The chorus of music rose and fell in symphonic cadence while the light danced in consonance to its sound. I could have remained a silent observer for an eternity without ever tiring, but more questions surfaced to the forefront.

"You keep calling him 'the one you know as Alfie.' Do you know him as someone different?

"Yes, I know him. I know him by a different name."

"What is it?" I asked.

"That is his and mine to know alone," the Father answered, beaming in affectionate delight.

"What do all these people here call him by?" I continued.

"No one is called in this place. They are known."

I allowed those words to inhabit another rest in our conversation as they settled in my soul. Once again the Father was giving language to a great truth I had somehow always known or subconsciously hoped for. In our world everyone allowed their title, job, or accomplishment to define who they were. If only we could be truly known, I thought to myself, with a vulnerability and openness as refreshing as a glacier-fed stream. I looked again at Alfie's wife and daughter in the distance. They were truly known here, but what was their story before coming to this place?

"The mother and daughter there, how did they come to be here?" I asked, suddenly becoming hesitant to learn the full story as I sensed, once again, an undertone of deep pain.

"Hatred and fear," the Father said. His voice somber.

My mind surged towards conclusions of the worst possible kind and I heard myself blurt out: "Was she killed?" A slight air of retribution evident in my voice.

"No doctor would give her the care that she needed. She was not helped though she could have easily been saved. Because of the color of their skin and their economic station, they were overlooked and they died." The Father stated somberly.

"How did this happen?"

"The woman died giving birth to her child. And because the child was not helped in her birth, she did not live long either. Of all the people in the world who could have found reason to hold resentment in their hearts, the man called Alfie would have done so quite comfortably. Instead, he chose to fall on me when his heart was breaking and did not allow the disease of hatred to take root in his life. He found healing in my song and in turn, it resonated and amplified into the lives of many others. This is how he has come to grow into such a great tree."

There was no judgement or anger in his tone. Although he did not elaborate, my mind busied itself with the work of filling in imaginary details of the story. It was a futile effort which didn't last long. The peace that surpasses all understanding was a powerful substance radiating from the Father, and I found myself once again enveloped in the crush of its embrace.

After another pause, the conversation turned as a new thought took shape in the forefront of my mind. It was a question I had not yet considered since my journey first started, but now as I focused my gaze back to the great tree rising before us I wondered about the origins of my own story.

"Father?" I started with some apprehension. "Do I have a tree of my own?"

"Of course."

"Will I get to see it?"

"You will," he said with eternal endurance and I could tell we were settling into another pause. But now my heart had been flooded with anticipation at his words and I became as eager as a child lying wide awake in the pre-dawn hours of Christmas morning.

"Will it be soon?" I asked, making a paltry attempt at sounding patient.

"The time is now," The Father replied with a joy-filled chuckle. "But I will not be the one to take you to it. My son will show you the way. Look. He is coming now." And he pointed in the direction of the tree.

As he said it I wondered how I had not noticed him among the crowd of people before. The burnishing glow radiating off of him was more brilliant than any other light emanating from the rest of the living things in sight. To behold his garment was more like trying to stare into the sun. The tunic he wore was white and reached down to his ankles. Again, I was astonished at the detail with which I could observe the things in this place. As I stared into the glow of his tunic I could make out the thread weave of intricate patterns in the fabric, though he still stood at a distance.

His dark brown hair fell serenely across his shoulders in contrast to the white of his garment, but still emitted a luminous glow from every strand. His face held the features of a Middle Eastern man with olive skin and a spruce beard. He hadn't yet looked in our direction as he was still gesturing and conversing with the small crowd of people gathered around him. They all laughed in riotous delight together as though they had just participated in some great lark or escapade. A small child still clung to his leg and was giggling. By his gestures I could tell he was in the midst of saying goodbye to the crowd. With both arms he quickly reached down for the boy stuck to his leg and heaved him up into the air in a fresh outburst of elated laughter. The boy landed back in his arms and embraced and kissed the man before being placed back on the ground to run back on his way. It was then that he turned and started in our direction and our eyes met for the first time.

I understood then why the world wrote songs about his eyes. Deep oceans. Columns of fire. Entire worlds spiraling deep within, both colliding and forming—always. All of those captivating attributes were there without limitation. But what struck me so profoundly was the fact that his eyes were brown. It was this simple human feature which revealed to me a wholehearted embrace of humanity to which he was fully bound. He wasn't just a man, of course. But to me, his brown eyes conveyed that he was just like me.

Every pillar of piety and religious regimen I had been taught to adhere to in the assent that I would be brought closer to God in their observance seemed to crumble like the forgotten stones of an ancient tower which men once built as high as the heavens. While humanity endeavored to become more like God buried within their places of worship and creeds, the Great God of the universe had become like me, deeply embodied within the confines and limitations of humanity and mortality.

My unravelling continued as the Son of the Father made his approach to where we both stood; his eyes continued to stay locked onto mine and draw me in. Another profound awareness awoke deep within my understanding and undressed my fears. Until this moment, every fear and anxiety I had ever experienced could have been explained or rationalized effortlessly. But as my eyes remained on his, I found within myself the arguments for fear dissolving like foreboding shadows which disappear entirely in the presence of resplendent light.

A thought occurred to me just then. Had I only caught a glimpse of his eyes before this time, I knew I would have lived an entirely different life. A life not absent of fear, but where it could be approached as a puddle to be tromped through on a rainy day, as opposed to the raging waterfall crashing into jagged rocks I had made it out to be.

When he finally drew near enough to touch, our coming together was as natural as a bird reconnecting with its shadow after alighting in a field under the afternoon sun. Without saying a word or hesitating, I was being brought into a great embrace in his arms. As he held me, I felt known and completely accepted.

"I am so glad to see you, my friend," he said while holding me tight. I stood there unable to move—not wanting to move. Any words I could have verbalized in response would have fallen short in describing the peace now flooding me on the inside like the warmth from a hot savory cider consumed on a brisk winter morning. It empowered the great disarming which continued to dismantle every fortified bastion in my heart.

We finally broke apart and he looked into my eyes once again. I felt as though there was not one area in my life hidden from his gaze. I stood exposed, unable to hide, like a deer accustomed to the shelter of thick forest dropped into a vast and open field. He saw all that I had said, thought and done—both the good and the bad. Yet evident in his eyes was an invitation into love like I had never known before. It was a love devoid of expectation. His love was fully given before the first man or woman ever contrived to earn it. It was an invitation into true acceptance and to finally find rest.

"We have a walk ahead of us," he said, turning his gaze towards the distance where a range of mountains rose tranquilly above the canopy of the trees. He turned towards them and started to walk in their direction. After a few paces he stopped, turned back and called out with a gesture of his hand, "Follow me."

I turned to ask the Father if he was coming with us, but he was no longer standing beside me. Yet the sense of his abiding presence still pulsed in the atmosphere as though I was being held in his arms. There was nothing left for me to do but to follow the one the Father had called his son. I quickened my pace until he and I were walking side by side across the soft meadow grass of the forest in the direction of the mountains.

Chapter 19: The Man with the Guitar

It was almost noon on Tuesday. Kate's patient was scheduled to be removed from life support sometime after three o'clock. The family had made arrangements for everyone to be there and they had been gathering all morning. These were all normal occurrences in the I.C.U. which she had been through with many other patients. But she had never cried so many tears as she had over this one. The family had embraced her both as a friend and daughter — and why? She didn't know Michael personally. She hadn't done a thing to improve her patient's condition. She didn't even know what to do with herself half the time as she stood helplessly by while the family held Michael's hand and wept.

She found herself contemplating the events of the morning when her shift first started. She had arrived early as promised and sat with Michael's sister for a time before having to transition to the charts and report with the nightshift nurse. The report was brief. She had busied herself with her routines and procedures as more family wandered through the room and conversed, hugged, and wept.

Most of them at this point would allow Kate to stay in the room with them while they sat beside their brother, nephew, conductor, and friend. Even Jessie at this point had warmed somewhat while still maintaining a safe distance from the friends and family all around her.

Jessie had come and gone a few times in the morning already and greeted Kate with a silent smile. Though she didn't speak to anyone her eyes told a story of heartache and grief. Her relationship with Michael had deteriorated and their marriage had ventured under the darkness of perilous cloud, but he was still the only man who ever said, 'I love you.' Now pulling the plug meant cutting the last thread of salvation keeping her from a lonely freefall into an endless abyss of depression and despair.

Michael's mom was back in the room just before noon and Kate was swallowed into a large family hug with Helen and Michael's sisters as the tears flowed freely, soaking into Kate's scrubs on both sides of her shoulders and arms. It was too much and before long Kate was excusing herself for a break and retreated into the comfort of obscurity in the hospital cafeteria on the main floor.

There she sat staring a hole through her half eaten toast, her mind tormented by the sights, conversations, and tears of a family preparing to say goodbye. What made everything that much worse was the voice and the words she had heard almost a month ago. She was certain by now there was no credibility to it and passed it off as a moment of wishful thinking—both the full recovery as well as the 'my daughter' piece that had moved her heart a month ago.

But like the faithful return of ocean tides she would find herself back in the moment she heard it—"My daughter"— and begin drowning once again in the churning of conflicted emotion, fragile faith, and implacable facts. What am I supposed to do with all this? She thought to herself.

Kate let the minutes pass while her thoughts clashed in jarring contention. The thought of returning early from her break to the maelstrom of emotions in the I.C.U. seemed more palatable than remaining lost in her tormented meditation.

She was about to get up from her spot when a stranger caught her attention and she held her place a few moments longer. There was something about him which provoked an inquisitive second look. He was a young dark-skinned man with a guitar slung loosely behind his back. He appeared to be similar in age to Kate, but carried himself with a confidence she had not readily observed among her peers. Accompanying him in front of the coffee station while they both filled their cups was a man she recognized as one of the hospital chaplains who had frequented the I.C.U. when called upon by a family. He was similar in age as well. They were laughing together like old friends. Kate caught herself glancing at the men's left hands—a routine examination for a single person as habitual as biting at a loose nail. A band on the chaplain's left hand revealed he was already happily married, but the stranger with the guitar wore no such designation. Further observation of the stranger revealed to Kate he was also very handsome.

Kate was about to dismiss this brief interruption and continue on her way when a presence seemed to drop down and envelop her in a sensation all too familiar, as when she first heard the voice. She was already half standing with her cafeteria tray in hand when the feeling returned and she paused in braced anticipation. The voice she had long discounted and never thought she would hear again— spoke to her heart once more.

"My daughter, ask him to play his guitar for your patient," It said. There was no mistaking it once again. It resonated as clear as an audible voice and filled her insides like a thick warm broth. Her racing heart and an accompanying shiver of adrenaline coursing through her was confirmation that her body heard it as well and was preparing to respond—or run away.

This can't be happening. I'm losing my mind, she thought to herself as she slowly stood the rest of the way with the tray still balanced precariously in her hands. Her feet felt welded to the floor and she froze while time slowed down, counted now by the beats of her heart which pounded audibly in her head.

She began to rationalize and feel for logic like it was a latch to a door which would free her from a dark room of uncertainty. She tried in vain to convince herself that it was just wishful thinking brought on by a fleeting moment of attraction to the opposite sex. Of course she wanted to believe this could be happening. Of course she wanted Michael to suddenly wake up. Of course she wanted to embrace an invitation into belonging, acceptance, and love which seemed to be the underlying force in the voice which unraveled all of her arguments and threatened to return her to tears.

Coffees in hand, the two gentlemen began to casually meander out of the cafeteria and into the atrium where they would most likely disappear into one of the myriad of hospital hallways. As she watched them go, she considered to herself that if she stood there long enough, perhaps the irritant of conviction she felt would dissipate as they disappeared from sight. She was not given the luxury to test this theory, however, as she felt her feet start to move beneath her involuntarily as soon as the two disappeared around the corner. It was as though she was being pulled along by a mysterious force like an invisible cord intertwined with three strands — faith, hope and love.

She discarded her tray by the exit and followed the men into the atrium. A sudden shock overcame her as she found herself closer to them than she anticipated. They had stopped to talk just around the corner and she found herself on a collision course with the spot where they stood, only a few feet away. Kate jumped as a wave of panic knocked her off course and she brushed past them only inches apart. As she did so, she risked a glance in the stranger's direction only to find her eyes meeting with his as he acknowledged her with a warm and inviting smile. Although Kate was not expecting that she managed a weak smile in return before she continued in her retreat.

She made a dash for the elevators, convinced she was going crazy with every additional step. All she had to do was get back to the safety of her floor and wait for whatever this was to pass like a bad headache. As she approached the main elevator corridor a welcome chime sounded and one of the doors opened, inviting her into its safety. Three others joined her in the car — a doctor along with a mother accompanying her young son who had a cast on his arm. Kate hit the button for her floor without turning around, preferring instead to keep her back to the doors while she waited for the sound to indicate they had closed. But the sound never came.

'What is taking so long?' she thought impatiently to herself. With a quarter turn of her neck she strained to see what could be delaying her departure. The mother had her finger pressed firmly against the door-open button. An additional turn was required to see what the holdup was. Kate faced the door and saw only a few feet away a frail and elderly woman shuffling slowly towards the open doors with her walker and an I.V. pole in tow. The nurse in her responded and stepped out to assist the woman with her pole in order to get her get into the elevator — and quickly. But the woman moved slower than a stagnant pond and Kate was tempted to give her a push if it could help her retreat any faster. Dismissing that thought with a roll of her eyes she inched her way beside her ward as they languidly crossed the elevator threshold. The waiting doctor looked annoyed.

Finally, with everyone on board, the mother could remove her finger from the button which had been stalling Kate's escape from the emotional drama she felt sure was self-induced. But as the doors finally began to close, the voice returned as audible and clear as a strong pulse. "My daughter," she heard it say. In a split second her arm shot into the bite of the elevator doors like a karate chop action toy in the hands of a child. Before she could process what was happening she was once again outside the elevator as the doors finally closed behind her. The doctor would have to assist the woman in the walker now.

Finding herself back in the atrium she retraced her steps to where the stranger with the guitar last stood. Scanning the whole area as she approached, a new uncertainty caused her to tense. What if that was my only chance to respond? She wondered. What if I blew my only opportunity to do something right? What if God is upset with me? The last question seemed to settle into her heart with a quivering chill. Years of subconscious irresolution around the nature and character of God had dug cisterns into which this reasoning fit perfectly. She continued to search the area, her growing anxiety feeding into her heightened resolve to recover her quarry and salvage the situation. But as if in response to a dormant expectancy, dejection set in as her search yielded no sight of the stranger with the guitar. He was gone.

He could have gone anywhere, swallowed up within the countless corridors and wards of Mt. Zion. She could feel the embroiling vehemence of arguments surface on both sides of her soul, throwing condemnation like rotten food—both for yielding to the voice and not yielding soon enough. They hammered down upon her like the clamoring of a judge's gavel. *Why am I such a failure?*

Hurriedly, she retreated to an unoccupied bench and buried her head in her hands. Tears welled up and spilled down the side of her face as her resolve released its final dying breath. She wiped at her tears which only made matters worse as her whole face flushed and ran with mascara from their overflow. As her sobbing carried on with an uncontrolled abandon a prayer was slowly germinating deep within the cracks of her broken faith. There, in the obscurity of the vast hospital atrium it sprouted and found Kate's voice in no louder than a whisper:

"God. I need your help." Her words exhaled into a faithless vacuum as she searched for more vocabulary to expound on her prayer. Finding none, her shoulders finally slackened as her tension and anxiety collapsed on the field of surrender. "Please help." Kate whispered under her breath. She hoped he would understand.

Through the echo and din of the atrium, the muted strum of guitar strings reached her ear as if in a gentle response to her plea. This did nothing, however, to stop the flow of tears as the feeling of relief washed over her. She sat there with her face still buried in her hands allowing the embrace of peace to settle and the tears to run their course. Once she regained her composure, she thought, she would follow the sound of the guitar in an adventure into the unknown. But not before first finding a washroom and cleaning up her face.

The guitar grew louder as Kate ventured down the hallway of the palliative care ward until she came to the source of the sound outside a patient's room. On top of the cadence of the guitar the stranger had a velvet voice and sang beautiful and enduring hymns. When the final refrain of the song hung softly in the air another voice, presumably the chaplains, moved in with a prayer. Following the prayer, gracious words of gratitude were exchanged in hushed tones before the pair stepped back out into the hallway. The stranger met Kate's eyes with a look of surprise and a step back, most likely not expecting to see someone standing right outside the door. But his smile told Kate that he was somehow happy to see her again.

"Hi. My name's Kate. I'm a nurse in the I.C.U.," she said, pausing long enough so the two could complete the introductions.

"Hi there, Kate. My name's Kyle."

"Sam. Nice to meet you," the chaplain said, politely extending his hand to Kate.

"I'm so sorry to sneak up on you guys like this, but I have a patient right now who's..." Her voice drifted off as she paused long enough to figure out what to say next. "Well, he's not doing well and today might be his last day. The family is all there and I was wondering if you might be able to come and play something?"

"Of course," Kyle said enthusiastically.

"Okay, great. Please follow me," Kate said now turning to lead them to the I.C.U. Sam and Kyle could not see the fresh look of apprehension that now appeared on Kate's face as she considered what she was going to tell the family when she showed up.

Chapter 20: My Father Who is in Heaven

We walked through meadow, forest, and field, side by side at all times. As we went, he never presumed to take a step beyond where I walked. We journeyed side by side. If I slowed to take in a sight, when I'd turn back, there he remained slowing or stopped, fully present with me wherever I was. Our walk seemed to occupy no measurement of time. It could have lasted only hours or spanned countless lifetimes. But it did not seem to drag on and my feet did not get tired.

We walked past other stumps with trees growing on them, all varying in size, none of which came close to the stature of Alfie's tree. And there were people, always people everywhere. Every last one was beautiful to behold. It was when my eyes would meet theirs, up close or from a distance, I would feel an immediate connection to the very essence of who they were even as I felt their gaze penetrating affectionately into depths I didn't know I possessed.

The words of the Father hung audibly over my thoughts: "No one is called in this place. They are known." Had I heard this statement in the world no amount of study and learning would have ever brought me close to comprehending its meaning. But as we journeyed on I felt like I was rejoining with long lost friends of the soul as they waved or greeted me with joyful laughter as effortlessly as a stream finds the ocean. Their eyes danced with elation and conveyed the same intimation: 'You're with him.'

It occurred to me that when my travel companion and I met, no

162

introductions were made. None seemed necessary at the time. The Father had simply indicated that he was his son. But our walk had been cultivating more questions within me which now seemed ripe for harvest and I wondered at how I would initiate them.

"Jesus?" I ventured, even though I knew it was him, although I also understood he was known by many names.

"Yes?" he said.

"Can you explain the trees to me some more? All the ones growing on top of stumps."

He smiled as though already anticipating the question. "Every tree growing in the deep roots represents a life. A soul. A cherished child." As he said it he paused, looking out at the vast expanse of the country we had been traversing. With a sweeping gesture of his arm, he continued. "Life begins here. It is where every soul is planted, where it belongs, and where it desires to return."

We continued to walk on in silence while his words settled like a mist over tranquil waters. Taking in my surroundings which inspired inexpressible awe was one thing. But where was 'here?' I wondered to myself. Did this place have a name? Or, like the inhabitants, was a place only known and perhaps not named? Again, answers from the arsenal in my Sunday school learnings confounded my thoughts with a simplistic knowledge I knew fell drastically short. We must have been in 'heaven' I thought, but even now as the blades of grass beneath our feet swayed with a rhythmic vibrancy which engaged all my senses, any name at all for a place like this seemed disparagingly inadequate.

"And where exactly are we?" I asked. "What do you call this place?"

Stopping again to answer and this time turning to face me he said, "In me."

Even as he said it, his words pulled on my heart like the effortless persuasion of gravity on an object. His words held a profound meaning; this much I knew, yet the words continued to elude full comprehension.

"If the trees growing here represent a life, why are they growing on stumps? Why couldn't they just grow up out of the ground like the rest of the trees of the forest?" I asked indicating at the forest draped across the terrain of hills and valleys.

"The trees of the forest which grow up out of the ground are only given the one path to follow and grow in response to me. They shoot up out of the ground and echo back the very song that gave them life. But the seeds of life for every child born of God are planted inside of me. They are invited to grow in and through me, in connection to the deep eternal roots."

"So you're the stump? We're all growing inside of you?" My questions continued to grasp at concepts my heart could embrace while my mind struggled to understand.

"All were given life inside of me. But not all accept the invitation to grow," he said with a subtle sadness.

I thought back to Alfie's tree. Its monumental heights defying all that I thought any living thing could possibly attain. It would take a thousand years or more for a tree in our world to ever caress the sky like that. "How does a tree grow here?" I asked.

"They grow in their connection to me and drink from streams accessible only to the deep roots beyond the boundaries of time and creation."

"Were the stumps always... um, stumps? Or were they trees once themselves?"

164

Returning my question with another he said, "When a tree is cut does it die?"

"Um… I think so?" I answered irresolutely.

Unless a tree is cut down and dies, it cannot open itself up to allow new life to grow inside of it. The shoot growing from a stump, though it is fragile, is already connected to roots that reach deep and take on the life of the tree that once grew in its place. It can draw from the springs of life far below while growing up on a foundation that cannot be moved. Every other tree of the forest starts life on the surface and can be uprooted by a falling branch or a gust of wind. My roots are eternal, reaching far beyond creation and time. And now so are yours, because of where you are planted."

"Where was I planted?"

"Come and see," he said.

I couldn't say how long our journey lasted. There was no way to count the days as I was soon to discover they were no longer distinguished by the setting of a sun. It wasn't until we had put some distance between ourselves and the foot of Alfie's tree that I realized there was no sun at all. The brilliant illumination engulfing us was being cast by the land itself. The sky sustained its own radiance with an effortless and eternal glow which fused itself to the resplendency of the terrain along the edge of the horizon. For what felt like days, Alfie's tree continued to rise in the background like a great tower of witness as we traversed fields, forests, and foothills. It wasn't until the cliffs from a mountain range, growing larger as we drew near, finally hid the enormous tree from view behind its ridgeline as we ventured deep into the embrace of its elevations.

Though we didn't converse much as we walked I never felt

alone in my thoughts. The company of my travel companion seemed to permeate my quiet introspection and reason. And the music! A sustained and harmonious sound was always there pitching like a tree in a gentle wind, transposing in rhythm and key as our feet accessed new heights in our climb into the mountains. It was as comforting as exultant laughter or cathartic tears shared in the company of close friends. I was certain now that the miles we covered would have taken weeks and required a small contingent of guides and pack animals to sustain our strength. But as the landscape changed and we walked on I never wearied or felt hunger. There could only be one reason for my unceasing vitality I thought as I continued in tireless stride: I was with him.

With a single word, we could have arrived wherever our destination was supposed to be. But Jesus chose the journey. And I could guess at why that may have been. The longer we walked together the more I felt myself becoming like him. Like an instrument transfigured into an expression of the one who plays it I found myself resonating with the thoughts and nature I knew to be his.

As we ventured further, it became just as much a process of un-learning the lies from my past. Truth began to blossom in my mind with refreshing clarity just as I found old logic and perceptions falling away into crumbles of dust like a meteor deteriorating in the atmosphere.

I heard the words again echoing from Pastor Steve's message spoken at my dad's funeral: "God does not create our pain. He walks through it, entering into it with us. It's why he sent his son Jesus to walk the dusty roads of humanity. God with us." As I walked with Jesus, it became impossible for me to comprehend how I had embraced the contrary as a disillusioned and hurting child. I was never abandoned to my pain— I was being held through it. It was quite the journey.

But I knew it was over when I saw the tree in the distance. It stood no higher than a street light including the stump at its base. Its canopy was sparse, still displaying the signs of young growth in its fragile branches which would not yet hold the weight of a man. It sat along the side of a babbling tributary stream in a mountain valley. The sound of flowing water echoed off the shoulder ridges rising on either side. A song emanating from the tree was the familiar music I had once heard from the choir of trees as a child and its melody reverberated pleasantly helped with the acoustics of the valley floor. I knew we had come to my tree.

A lone figure sat with his back resting against the trunk. As we approached from a distance, I could see his stunned reaction as he became aware of our arrival in the valley. The man stood slowly, all the while keeping his riveted gaze fixed on us as we drew near. It was likely the man found himself transfixed in the same wonder I experienced when seeing Jesus approaching for the first time. But he was equally captivated when his eyes rested on me. There was a subtle hint of familiarity in his gaze like a cherished scent from home awakening the senses in a foreign country. This man was no stranger to me. When only a short distance remained between us I heard him speak.

"Michael!" He said in a whisper of longing affection.

I stopped in my steps fixed motionless to the ground.

"Dad?"

"He told me you were coming," my dad said, his arms opening in invitation as he had done so many times before. My heart and feet leapt in the same instant causing me to break away from the ground and run into his embrace. Though in appearance he exuded the touch of ethereal transformation, in his arms I felt his gentle strength, which I had known so well, wrap around me like the supple leather of a well-worn glove. We remained together while Jesus looked on from a few steps behind, neither of us wanting to let the other go.

I felt the first lone tear navigate a moist path down my cheek. There was a pain rising to the surface from a place deep inside. One which lay dormant and buried under a lifetime of evasion as impenetrable as a granite wall. The first crack appeared at the sight of my dad. Further tectonic shifts ensued as he held me in his arms. The eruption was coming.

"Why did you have to leave?" My question, muffled by his shoulder expressed itself in a tormented bellow giving way for the others to follow. "You promised you would come home! You promised!" More tears began to flow making new and wider paths down the sides of my face like the rising waters of a swollen river. "Why did you have to leave?" I asked again with a sharper tone, a hint of rising anger like steam permeating from the peak of a mountain.

I was a twelve-year-old boy again in that moment sitting at my father's funeral. The sound of the bell ushering in a hollow new reality of fatherlessness assailed at my heart until it hung lifeless and broken like a mutilated body nailed to a tree. I remembered hearing the volley of the guns in the distance and how it galvanized my resolve to embrace the rising outcry of rage and indignation then amplified by each report.

"God's not good."

BANG!

"God doesn't care about you."

BANG!

"You're alone."

BANG!

Still holding my dad in my arms, I turned to face the one I had blamed all my life for the pain I held inside — surprised now by its sudden resurgence after a long and life-changing journey through heaven and earth at his side. But Jesus, no longer standing off at a distance where I left him, had drawn closer to where my dad and I stood. It startled me to see him up so close, but it completely unraveled me to see his face.

An effusion of tears washed down the sides of his visage from eyes which conveyed a deep sorrow and mirrored the intense suffering I felt inside. The remaining residual of resistance which had maintained any doubt about his love fell silent like the peaceful hush of armistice settling upon a tranquil field after the guns had fired their final shots. Jesus was weeping — for me. I didn't have to tell him a thing. His eyes told me everything. He knew my pain and it mattered deeply to him. He was not the cause of my hurt or the architect of my anguish — he had entered into it with me. God with us!

At my father's funeral, while others around me could engage with their heart and emotions, I was constructing walls around my heart while numbing my pain with anger. But in my mind's eye, I could see myself once again sitting silently, but no longer alone. I saw Jesus there. Standing behind me and leaning over with his arms curled around my chest, he wept until my hair became saturated with his tears like a healing oil washing over my soul.

Sensing a reprieve settling, I volunteered my voice to break the silence.

"I thought there were no tears in heaven?" I asked, making an effort to end my question with a grin.

I heard my dad offer a light chuckle and Jesus smiled in return. "That day has not come. For I have yet to make all things new. But I can do this." With that, he leaned in towards me and with his hands, wiped the waning flow of tears from my eyes while they still rolled freely from his. His touch was gentle, but his hands were calloused and felt rough against my face. Again, I was struck by his humanity in that moment. Of course! I thought to myself, he was a carpenter after all.

He then reached for my hands and placed them against the roots of my tree. I was startled as I made contact to feel heat radiating from the base as though I had just touched a sick child burning with fever. I flinched but Jesus held my hands steady in his.

"Your tree is sick and has not grown for some time," he said, looking at the roots. I followed his stare and noticed a thin black and grey crust growing around the base of the tree like a slick of oil resting on the surface of water. "The disease runs deep," he said, his eyes now meeting mine. His look was somber, but never lost its invitation into grace.

I didn't know what to think. I continued to study my tree for a while with a mute inquisitiveness. First tears and now disease? My misconceptions about God and eternity were being laid bare like thin sheets on a laundry line made transparent against the sun.

"Can it get better? Can it grow again?" I asked.

"This is why I have brought you here," he said and paused before continuing. "A tree will only produce new songs while it grows. Your tree has many more songs to sing. What you have heard and known so far has only been the outcome of its young growth—melodies and rhythms from the fresh scent of leaves. There is still fruit to come which you have not yet tasted or seen."

"My tree can grow fruit?" I wondered out loud to myself in a soft whisper. I remembered the clusters of figs growing on Alfie's tree, its great heights and the large community drawn together by its beautiful song. It was hard to imagine that the young, fragile and diseased tree in contrast before us could ever come close to such an exulted potentiality.

"It can and it will." Was Jesus' confident response. "But first, you must heal and re-establish connection with the ancient roots in which you were first planted. You cannot grow outside of me."

My thoughts traversed back through my experiences since my collapse on the stage. My wife? Travis Bishop? Alfie? My dad? And now this sick tree? I suddenly felt overwhelmed as though caught within a strong current which had finally pushed me into the retreats of a waterfall's edge. With no strength remaining to swim against the flow, I was preparing to be swept over.

"This is all getting to be a bit too much. What am I supposed to do with everything I've seen?" I asked.

"I've shown you these things so that you would know me. I want you to see as I see and know my heart. My heart for your wife, Travis, Alfie, your dad, and you," he said reassuringly.

I slumped and looked down again at my tree. My thoughts drifted off to my first memories of its song as a young child which awakened me to the life I lived—or at least the life I thought I lived. I recalled the potent anxiety which surfaced as Paul Waverley from *Vanity Fair* posed his penetrating questions on the day of my collapse. "If I asked you if your best days were still ahead, what would you say to that?" The question picked at an aggravating vacancy in my life like a scab that refused to heal.

"So how does the tree heal?" I asked.

"A great exchange," Jesus said. "You will have my joy, if you will give me your sorrow. You will have my peace if you will give me your pain. You will have my hope, if you will give me your disappointment. Instead of ashes, you will have a crown. Instead of mourning, I will wrap you in a celebration song."

His words imparted warmth like an invitation to rest by a fire after stepping in from the cold. "This all sounds great—but how do I actually give you what you're asking for? If I had anything in my hands right now I would gladly give it, but I don't."

Jesus's eyes then drifted over to my dad. Together, they exchanged a knowing look which unsettled me like a misstep along the edge of a precipice. Jesus turned back to me and began to unravel another mystery.

"You father has been waiting here for you since the time he first arrived," he said.

"But my dad died over ten years ago. You mean he's been waiting here for that long?" I asked incredulously.

"There is no more the presence of time than there is the presence of darkness in this place. Your father has only just arrived." He spoke as though my dad had just stepped off a train. At that, my dad interjected.

"This is the only place I've seen since being here, son. When I arrived, the Father met me here and we spoke for a while. It was the most beautiful conversation I have ever experienced. He told me things too wonderful to imagine or believe, but I know it is true. When we finished talking, he told me to wait here because his son would soon be coming with my son. It was not long after that I saw you both coming in the distance."

Jesus placed his hands on my shoulders and looked deep into my heart. I could feel his eyes piercing the source of my greatest pain and felt my lips quiver and fresh tears swell up in anticipation for what I sensed was coming.

"The time has come for the great exchange and the healing of your tree." Michael, your father must come with me now. There is a great journey that lies ahead of us and I must show him all that my Father has promised."

"NO!" The vehemence of my cry broke across the mountain valley with the magnitude of a volcanic eruption. In an instant, I had broken away from Jesus and collapsed on my dad, seizing him in my arms as though his existence depended on my grip. "You can't have him!" I cried. "You've already taken him from me once!" I shouted between sobs which roiled like a turbulent sea.

"Michael, will you now give me what you hold in your hands in exchange for what I have promised to give you?" Jesus asked with grace and eternal patience.

"No! I don't want him to go! *I* don't want to go! Why can't we both stay here together?" I protested while continuing to hold fast to my dad with feverish misery. I felt my dad's hand rest on my head and I could tell that he was crying, the sound of a sniffle conveying his own emotion.

Jesus continued to articulate in a tender tone. "Michael, your time has not yet come. There is a beautiful sound yet to be woven into the fabric of your world that will flow from the place of your healing. Will you give me your father and trust that I am good?"

I sobbed in abandon with heaving convulsions that shook my body while I clung to my dad and soaked his chest with a fresh outpouring of tears. I held him while my heart broke again along the same fissure where it had first been torn in two. I wailed and moaned with audacious liberty while the pain flowed raw and unrestrained until I thought my entire being would vanish with the outflow — and still more came.

The cry of my broken heart reverberated through the corridor of the valley walls around us. I felt the touch of Jesus's hand on my back while I lingered in my grief. Having found the gift of release, I mourned my father like I wished I could have the day I sat at his funeral. Together the three of us stood while my cathartic ablution ran its course and the raging river of my broken heart slowed to a quiet stream still churning with sporadic whimpering trembles. I felt no constraint of time while we all huddled together and I radiated with the slow burn of my purge like a hot coal buried in the sand.

After another eternity had passed, Jesus spoke: "I will have your dad with me, but you will always have mine with you. He has promised never to leave you and never to forsake you."

"I know," I said, feeling resigned to the peace which now covered me like a blanket.

"Will you let your father come with me now?" He asked again with compassion.

"I know I have to, but it's still hard to let go. It really hurts," I admitted.

"I know your pain, but I hold your joy. Here, rise up and stand before me."

My grip around my father eased and my arms slowly returned to me. I stood, turning around and faced the one who had journeyed with me to this place. I noticed in his hands he held a clay jar. It had a simple smooth, round base with a fluted, narrow top and a single handle formed at its side.

"This is the first of many more gifts you will receive from me," he said as he removed a cork stopper from its top, releasing a profusion of beautiful fragrance into the air. Lifting the jar above my head he tipped it, allowing an oil to flow freely and cover my head like a lustrous crown. It continued to drip down to my shoulders and soak into my clothes, touching my skin with a soothing cool. The baptizing balm felt light to my heart awakening a youthful vigor from my past like the arousing memory from a first kiss. Courage and joy surged through my body like a deep ocean fills a fissure when it forms along its bottom, filling the cavernous wasteland of my sorrow until it was submerged in gentle peace.

I felt the presence of my dad as he stood to his feet close behind me. I turned to him and fell on his shoulders again in an embrace. "I love you so much," I said, no longer able to access the stabbing pain which I had carried embedded in my soul. It was gone, removed like an infected sliver. There was a freedom accompanying the knowledge that I could let him go.

"I love you, son. You'll never be alone. And I will be here waiting to see you again," he said.

Over his shoulder, I caught a glimpse of my tree once again and was drawn to its base. The sickness had already begun to recede. Where the black and grey film had previously enveloped the entire bottom half of the trunk, fresh patches of life had broken through and were advancing across the tree the way a bright orange glow of a smoldering burn slowly consumes a paper without a trace of flame.

"Apparently you have an adventure ahead of you. I wish I could go with you," I said to my dad as I took a step back, releasing him to the company of Jesus.

"You will be together again soon. But there is an adventure that still awaits you in the world where you must return. Remember, I will be with you always," Jesus said.

My dad walked to Jesus's side and together they turned to face the mouth of the valley and started their descent back along the trail that had brought us to my tree. After a few paces Jesus stopped and turned back to face me one last time.

"You will know it is time for you to go when you hear the music from your world once again," he said before resuming his journey with my dad across the valleys and mountains we had crossed. I watched them go until their shrinking figures disappeared behind the slope of the valley floor. It had gone quiet, but I knew I wasn't alone.

Chapter 21: Music from another World

The elevator ride up to the fourth floor seemed like an eternity. There was no exchange of conversation between Kate and the two strangers as her mind raced with the preoccupation of her next steps which still eluded her. *What the heck am I doing?* She could hear herself screaming inside. The tone signaled they had arrived at their floor and the elevator doors opened, triggering adrenaline to course through her even faster.

They stepped off and proceeded down the hall towards Michael's room where the family was gathering to say goodbye. Outside the room in the hallway a lineup of relatives and friends stood. Their tear-stained faces and somber expressions told Kate that their goodbye's had already been spoken. They waited outside while others did the same, tarrying together in the agony of the inevitable.

Kate stepped into the open doorway with two figures and a guitar following close behind her. Helen and Michael's three sisters sat in the room in a huddle around Michael's lifeless body, anointing him in their tears. Jessie sat in the room as well in a chair against the wall projecting a hollow stare onto the machines by her husband's side which would soon fall silent. Evidence of her own grief and exhaustion lingered in blushed stains and dark lines on her face.

Helen looked up at Kate and acknowledged her warmly. "Hi Kate. Please join us if you like," she said in a cracking, hollow voice.

"Oh Helen, I'm so sorry to intrude on you like this. This

gentleman is going around the wards with our chaplain playing guitar and I was wondering if you might want to have a few songs played in the room? I'm so sorry. I know I should have asked before bringing them here but..."

"That would be lovely," Helen answered graciously, acknowledging the chaplain and Kyle who stood behind her. The heads of Michael's sisters didn't turn to look up and Jessie remained motionless, turning only briefly to acknowledge the new people in the room before returning to her vacant stare and her silent contemplation of where she would go when this was all over.

Kate stepped off to the side of the room allowing Sam and Kyle to enter in. Without words, Sam greeted Helen with compassionate eyes while Kyle gently removed his guitar from its case.

The strumming from the guitar was delicate and ushered a peaceful calm into the room. There was no rush in Kyle's rhythm. With his eyes closed and fingers deftly pulling upon strings and hearts alike, he communed with his audience of One. No one else watched Kyle except for Kate from the corner of the room. Her nerves had been shot only moments before by the thought of facilitating what now seemed so natural and right. Mixed into her internal drama was the element of attraction which only undermined her resolve until now. A tear streamed freely through Kyle's closed eyes while he strummed and began to sing transcendently to a God who enveloped him in lovingkindness.

"When peace like a river attendeth my way. When sorrows like sea billows roll..."

His song and words flowed out of connection to his muse with an unconstrained liberty and effervescence drawing Kate into a desire to know him and the One he sang to more. The room remained captivated in the freedom of the moment for a time while

178

the songs and melodies ran their course, echoing through the hospital hall causing those nearby to draw closer to its source. There was a transposition of key followed by familiar lyrics, but everyone in the room suddenly felt a change in the atmosphere. Kyle began to sing the old hymn:

"Amazing grace how sweet the sound. That saved a wretch like me. I once was lost but now I'm found. Was blind but now I see."

A subtle shift broke upon the room like the first hint of dawn pulling the outline of the trees out of hiding against the backdrop of a night sky. Though it would have been impossible to trace the sound's path, its refrain passed through hospital walls and eternal tapestries alike until it could be heard echoing across a mountain valley occupying another space tucked between the folds of heaven and earth.

It reached my ears where I sat in the grass by my tree and startled me to hear such a conventional hymn in a place where music seemed to take on new expressions unrestrained by the limitations of tempo or tone. I stood to my feet and looked around straining to see some indication of the source but nothing moved or stirred. I stood for a time allowing the litany to wash over me like holy water calling to me from another life until I felt the sudden wave of exhaustion hit.

I had not known hunger, pain, or fatigue while walking with the Father or travelling in this place, but suddenly my body began to succumb to a weariness quickly overwhelming my entire being. I felt the sudden urge to lay down and rest and with a yawn I settled back down in the grass. My eyes became so heavy they could no longer remain open while the tune of "Amazing Grace" continued to roll over me like a gentle lullaby. My soul in heaven was fast asleep in the same miraculous moment my body in a New York hospital bed began to stir back to life. I was waking up.

Part III

Chapter 22: Recovery

As soon as the story of my awakening got out, media headlines everywhere began calling it "The Miracle of Music." When I stirred back to life, so did the rest of the hospital, humming like a hive of bees. Not only was my recovery in itself inexplicable, but the way in which I came back from the precipice of mortality drew the attention of medical professionals and media alike from all over the country.

Everyone was clamoring for their chance to observe, analyze, and interview the one who had been pulled back from the brink of certain death and whose brain grew back through the "coincidence" of a simple song. Indeed that is the story every M.R.I. and brain scan told. Where the bleed from the aneurism had caused swelling and atrophy all of the images were now showing a perfectly normal and healthy human cerebrum. This story would be making waves for some time—and they didn't know the half of it, I thought.

My recovery was not instant, however, as my time in a hospital bed being fed by tubes had left me frail and weak. I had lost almost thirty pounds and was not overweight to start with. I was still going to be in the hospital for a while working on gaining my weight and muscle strength back. They moved me to a larger private room where I was slowly introduced to liquids before graduating to a gelatinous gruel with a Plasticine aftertaste.

The physiotherapy was not something I looked forward to either. Twice a day, I was ushered into a different area on the ward to be subjected to various exercises and routines designed to stimulate my core and muscles which had laid dormant for so long.

Although it was not altogether completely unpleasant, it was a harsh new reality to grow accustomed to after the experience of heaven.

I was not without help. My mother practically never left my side throughout the weeks of my recovery and was as protective as an eagle guarding her nest of young. The visitors all vying for an audience with me had to get past her first. Even the physicians running their tests were subject to her scrutiny and learned an efficiency which cut back on their elective examinations.

The only medical professional it seemed who could circumvent my mother's watchful eye was the nurse named Kate. I remembered her right away from my journey through the hospital with the Father. I learned how she had been one of my regular nurses while in my coma and observed how my mother seemed to welcome her into my room for visits as naturally as if she were one of her own daughters. Although she was a stranger to me, it did not take long for my admiration to grow for her as well. Kate's visits were frequent but short and often involved only a brief hello on my part while she fraternized with my mother or sisters when they were in the room.

I remember the day I met Kyle. Of course he was in the room on the day I awoke to his acoustic medley of "Amazing Grace," but my awakening was like venturing into a heavy fog after days of travelling through a sunlit field. I had been immediately inundated by frenzied family members and doctors alike while I lay disoriented and debilitated for days after my return. I never really met Kyle until one week later when Kate appeared in my room with him by her side.

Though they did not walk in holding hands, I noticed right away a spark of affection connecting the two of them together. Their nervous laughter and glances at each other were all signs of a young romance as fragile and vibrant as the new growth of spring buds. But as he broke away to engage in conversation at my bedside I felt an immediate bond with the man who had serenaded me as I woke up. His eyes flashed with a captivating wholeness reminiscent of Jesus's gaze and I succumbed to an immediate wave of emotion. "No one is called in this place… they are known."

Tears were flowing before I could even manage a word. As if in response to my silent acknowledgment of the soul, a mirrored response of moisture gathered in his eyes before cresting and falling onto my bedsheets as he leaned in to give me a hug. We stayed together in an embrace for a drawn-out moment while our muted sniffles were the only sound in the room.

"Thank you," I said. My voice was muffled by his shoulder still in my face. "Your music is beautiful."

Kyle gave out a light chuckle in mild protest. "You have no idea what that means coming from someone like yourself. Thank you." He slowly withdrew from our embrace.

As he sat back upright at the side of my bed, we both said nothing for a while. Our knowing glances said more than an hour of conversation could have ever revealed. Though both musicians in our own right, there was a deeper connection, a shared experience somewhere in our past. In the window of each other's souls we both saw the familiar face of Jesus — the one whom we had come to know and love when he stepped into our darkest pain with the light of hope. And it was beautiful.

Eventually we settled into conversation and spoke of our music and pasts. He told stories of his grandfather and his first guitar while I recounted memories of pianos and violins at the age of three and four.

"Kyle," I began after some time in conversation had passed, "did you happen to bring your guitar with you?"

His eyes lit up in response to the question. "You bet I did!" he said and immediately disappeared into the hall. He returned only seconds later with his guitar case in hand. I didn't have to ask him to play. Before I could say another word, Kyle had his Fender positioned across his lap and began strumming whimsically with his eyes closed, already lost in the rhythm of the riff.

Kate had settled deeper into the only other chair in the room as one already familiar with the journey Kyle was leading us on. Her eyes were closed and a subtle smile crept across her face. I was struck again by her beauty, both outwardly and deep within. She exuded compassion and grace in her interactions with my family leaving me longing for the depth I knew was lacking in my own life which had stretched miles wide and inches deep. Kyle was right to pursue such a treasure if my suspicions were right.

I closed my eyes and immediately saw Jessie's face. Since waking up I had only seen her briefly a handful of times. She appeared distracted at each visit, often staring blankly through a wall off to the side of my head. I tried to hold her hand a few times, but she recoiled as if my hands were a hot element on a stove. I spoke nothing of my experiences in heaven or of her affair. Our few conversations were short and strained.

Surprisingly, I could not access the anger or hurt I thought I might feel. Was it even there at all? Every time I thought about the affair, the image of the little girl with a doll in her hand and terror in her eyes would steal upon me, breaking my heart all over again.

Kyle's music continued to reverberate in soft, flowing tones whisking each listener deep into the place of the heart. With my eyes still closed I heard Jesus's words which had been spoken around my tree: "Your tree has many more songs to sing." The words began to intertwine with the newly thriving compassion for my wife like wisteria scaling a stone wall, and I wondered about her own tree growing in the roots of eternity. Like mine, it too would most likely be sick, throbbing with the heat of disease cultivated by a lifetime of pain. What was Jessie's song the Father was singing over her? If only she could hear its melody again.

The refrain from the final note hung in the air as Kyle's song came to an end and it was quiet for a time. The distant din of hospital activity crept its way back through the half-open door of my room, reminding me again of my institutional environment. I had not yet felt the yearning for freedom from my twenty-four hour care which held me captive, but as ideas began to blossom I felt the pull of inspiration calling to me from beyond the sterile walls.

"Kyle, that was beautiful," I said. "We should write music together one of these days."

Chapter 23: Rude Awakenings

Two evenings later I sat up in my hospital room with Jessie sitting in a chair at my side. We made our regular attempts at small talk. My health, my family, her fitness classes. I learned long ago asking about her own family was a topic which remained strictly off limits, so there was never any discussion there. Silence filled the spaces in between our intermittent discussion and her eyes remained fixed on the wall behind me as if it were a transparent window of escape. Rarely did our eyes ever meet. It had been like this for as long as I could remember.

In the space of another silence, after all possible avenues of discussion had been shallowly traversed, the words I had been contemplating for this moment rose to the surface. I glanced at one of the monitors reading my heart rate off to the side. It was accurately reporting my elevated pulse coursing within. Jessie did not notice.

"Jessie," I ventured in a softened tone. "Look at me please."

Jessie hesitated in evident discomfort.

"Please," I said. "This is important."

Slowly her eyes rose to meet mine after another passive pause. Over the years I had known my wife, her eyes revealed very little. They would flash when enraged or flirt when aroused. There had been a few moments of childlike wonder early in our relationship when she had truly been captivated by my music and those moments gave me a thrill. But she hid sadness behind the fortifications of her heart and closed bedroom doors. And love? We spoke the words to each other once, but I don't know if her eyes ever told me she loved me, nor had mine ever told her the same.

But now in her eyes I could see through her high walls to a depth I had never before witnessed and I ventured in as though treading on holy ground. Her heart held an ocean of sadness upon which a six-year-old girl floated on a crippled raft through turbulent storms and barren stillness. Alone. Afraid. Betrayed. A flood of emotion swelled from deep within me, tightening in my throat and misting my eyes as I began to speak.

"Jess. I know you're having an affair."

The words crashed upon her with a sobering impact. Her reaction was visceral; her whole body tensed while her eyes widened in fear and disbelief. She winced as though bracing for the next volley, a death blow to finish her off. They were words she had been expecting— words she knew she deserved to hear. But they never came.

"Jessie. I'm so sorry," I said, with vulnerable sincerity.

My words and emotion shook her and the first single stone began to fall from the parapet of her fortified heart. Her look of disbelief betrayed an inner desire to hear more of what I had to say.

"I'm sorry," I continued, "because I have not shown you the love that you deserve."

Tears fell in a straight line down my face as my words flowed from a well I had never drawn from before. "And I'm sorry for the pain I have caused you."

I let each statement settle in the silence before continuing with another. Her eyes slowly began to mist as they remained fixed on mine.

"I don't know the pain or the sadness of your heart. But while I was in my coma I met someone who does. I don't expect you to believe everything, but please hear what I have to say."

Another pause.

"I never believed there could be a God of love watching over us while so much suffering ran rampant and free through our broken and messed up lives. But we're broken and messed up because most of us have forgotten who he is and where we come from."

A tone over the hospital intercom interrupted as a clerk called out a code. It repeated twice in blaring monotony. Jessie and I sat motionless except for her nervous hands fidgeting with a string on her hoodie. I waited for silence again before I went on.

"But I saw him, Jess. God is real—and he's good. He's so good! There is a love fighting for us, surrounding us and singing over us that flows from his heart towards ours. But our pain and anger keep forcing it out and we believe we're all alone. I've felt that way most of my life and I know you have too."

Tears flowed freely cresting over in a current from our eyes as a tangible presence of peace descended in the room like a whisper.

"He doesn't cause our pain. He's in our pain with us contending for our hearts wanting to heal them. I know you've cried yourself to sleep at night. I've heard you—and so has he. He's seen your pain and is angered and broken over it. But he won't leave you there. It doesn't have to be the end of your story."

I could sense a storm churning up her ocean of sadness with buffeting gales from the past, as discomfort contorted her face in visible lines. I had seen that face many times before. She was building up for a fight—or a flight.

"He's never going to leave you. And Jessie, listen to me. Neither am I. I want to learn how to love you the way the Father has shown me how to love. If you'll stay with me, I promise I will always stay with you."

Those were the last words I said before she stood to her feet with a concentrated force of will while tears still washed down her face in an undignified blend of mascara and blush. Still sniffling she reached for her purse and turned towards the door before walking out without hesitation or a word. I could hear her muted sobs fade down the hospital hallway until it was silent again and she was gone.

Prayer was a new concept for me after so many years of silence between myself and 'the man upstairs.' I had not spoken to God since the day my dad died and it took near death on my part for the conversation with God to rouse again. It helped, of course, to have the physical form of the Father standing where I could touch and see him and hear his voice. Conversations with him now were going to be different, requiring more faith on my part. But I was up for this new endeavor. Everything had changed after I woke up. I knew I would never be alone again. The Father—my Father—was with me. Always.

I forgot that I had ever owned a Bible, but the sky-blue leather bound copy with my name inscribed in silver letters found its way into my room. It had been a gift to me when I was a child and mom brought it with her from home. It sat on a side table with a few of my childhood stuffed animals and old instruments in the corner of the room—the makings of a memorial. But when I was strong enough to sit up and hold objects in my hands with my own strength, I began to read through its pages once again.

I started in John. I recalled the few times in my past a family member or old friend with good intentions would encourage me to read the Bible. They would often say to me, "Just start with John." I had never expected such an encounter when I began to read. The first time Jesus referred to God as 'his Father,' I felt the swelling of emotion and a broach of tears flare up unexpectedly. The words came to life as they told a story I had experienced firsthand. Had I known how many times Jesus would reference 'his Father' in John, I probably would have started with a different book of the Bible all together.

The letters in red seized my heart like a starving man grappling for a loaf of bread. Tears fell across them in drops leaving a trail of wrinkled pages as I read along. At every prayer and reference to the Father I closed my eyes and could see His deep and piercing eyes penetrating my depths with ferocious love. I could feel the longing of Jesus to make his Father known to his disciples and the crowds. And now, here I sat wrestling and burning with the same desire.

How would I begin to tell people where I had been and what I had seen? The miracle of my recovery had certainly created an atmosphere where the concept of God was naturally brought up. Outside of God there was no medical or objective basis to explain the spontaneous regeneration of a brain. But no matter how magnificent the miracle, I found that some people still believed what they wanted to believe. If there was no room for God in their view of the world, the unexplained was merely an inconvenience to their otherwise resolute perspective on subjective truth. For those in the community of faith, my miracle worked to galvanize their conviction. But for me, the real miracle had taken place in my heart, which was now replete with peace like I had never known. Joy, too, seemed to percolate constantly close to the surface fueled by a newly kindled fire eternally burning in the deep of my soul. And people began to notice.

191

"You're different Michael." So many of my friends and colleagues said this after a visit to my bedside, calling out the change with an inquisitive look in their eye. Perhaps, I began to wonder, the change was all they were meant to know. So much of my heavenly encounter carried such a personal dynamic, like a tailor-fitted suit which would sag or distend in awkward places if worn by anyone else. After a time of settling into the new normal myself, I began to grow content with my demeanor speaking for itself, while I cherished and held my experiences close to my heart.

But there were a select few I wanted to share my story with—and my mother was the first. She sat with me one evening after my sisters had left the room on their final visit before returning to their homes. There were more lines across her face since the last time I had seen her. Grief and worry had added years and eroded her vitality like a constant drip carving into a rock over time. She was constantly tired, but an embedded contentment fed a glow of joy still radiating outwards and highlighting an inner beauty which had never left her after all these years. And now having come through my experience, the source she remained deeply rooted within was now obvious to me.

I exhaled in a contented smile once our regular small talk subsided and knew it was time to tell her the things her heart had always known.

"Mom, there's something you need to know," I said, while reaching forward to hold her hand in mine.

She didn't say anything but looked up to meet my eyes in quiet anticipation. That was my sign to continue.

"While I was in my coma, I was fully awake somewhere else."

Mom's eyes widened slightly. I could tell her mind already began racing towards the conclusion of our eternal hope.

"Mom, I met him—The Father. I met God the Father." Before the words were even out I found I had ventured into a crossroads branching off into the thousand possible directions of what to say next and paused to consider my next words. How could I begin to describe all that I had encountered? What was it my mom needed to hear the most? She leaned in closer to my bed and tensed as though her palpable expectancy could help draw my words out faster.

"He's been with me this whole time. I see that now. A single second with him could change a life forever, but he made time stand still altogether to show me the virtues of his nature and the thoughts of his heart; towards me, and towards others in my life. I saw beauty and heard melodies too wonderful to imagine and it all comes from him. He took me through moments of life and showed me perspective and how much higher his thoughts are than mine." I chuckled at this lightly. "I mean, it's one thing to hear this, but it's another thing all together to know."

My mom listened intently to every word as I attempted to articulate my experiences. I knew my retelling could only convey what our limited minds could comprehend and felt like a toddler trying in vain to replicate a Rembrandt with crayons. How could I even begin to explain the trees and the stumps? But the stories of my journey with God warmed her heart all the same and my words were welcomed with a restorative repose which eased slowly across her countenance, relaxing the lines on her face. I told her nothing of what I learned about Jessie and left the stories of Alfie out. Nothing could be gained in their telling. I came then to the part I knew she would want to hear the most.

"Mom, he took me to Jesus. And standing side by side with the two of them you can't help but notice a distinct resemblance in their features." Another light chuckle under my breath interrupted the thought. "It was like staring at that photo with me, Dad, and Grandpa — only a lot brighter and too wonderful for words. They're actually Father and Son, even in appearance!"

I spoke as one waking from a dream, recalling my experience in measured inflection and heartfelt language. But now, venturing close to the end of my journey, I felt a constriction in my throat lending a quiver of emotion to my voice while a reservoir of tears drifted imminently close to the surface.

"Jesus took me on another journey and we travelled together a long distance. I knew we had arrived when I saw someone standing off in the distance, waiting for us to arrive." And with that my reservoir spilled over in a cleansing wash of poignant tears. "And that's where I saw him. Dad was waiting for us there. I saw Dad. He's there, Mom. With Jesus."

The words broke upon her heart like a flash flood over parched land. A steady stream of tears welled and fell from her eyes. There had never been any doubt in her mind where her husband ended up, but to hear her deepest hope validated through my account was more than she had ever hoped to hear in this life. And it was all I needed to tell, or could tell, for that matter.

Mom dropped her head into her arms across my lap while I sat upright in my bed. My hand rose and fell with her heavy sobs as it rested gently on her back. Her heart healed with every tear that soaked the blanket covering me in the bed. If my journey across heaven and earth yielded only this moment at my return, I would have been content. But there was much more to come from it in the days which lay ahead.

Chapter 24: Homecomings

Six weeks after waking up I found myself standing back in my apartment, which stirred up feelings reminiscent of stepping into a dream. The last time I had stood in my bedroom, both nightmare and reality had collided in a surreal tempest of anger and pain when I had witnessed Jessie's affair. But now, as I walked back into our room no trace of her remained. The dirty laundry, which regularly littered her side of the bedroom, had been picked up and was gone. None of her clothes were left hanging in our closet and her side of the bathroom sink had been emptied. I searched every room, looking for any sign hinting at her possible return or even her whereabouts, but there was no evidence for hope in my half-emptied apartment — not even so much as a note.

I had called her countless times and left an accumulation of texts since the day she left my side suddenly at the hospital. Wherever she had gone she did not want to be found. I looked at my phone again in the vain hope that she had responded in the last hour, but my last text to her still sat at the bottom of our thread unanswered:

"I'll be home soon. I hope to see you there. There's so much more to say and I just want to talk. In the meantime, know that I love you no matter what."

Before my collapse, and heavenly encounter, an empty apartment would have been welcomed as a gift. When we were home together most of our time was spent in separate rooms. It was the path of least resistance. If we were together for any prolonged amount of time, an outburst or brawling exchange was inevitable—

and we had both grown tired of the routine.

But now the solitude ate away at my heart like the atrophy which had eroded the very cells of my brain and rendered me void of life. A love for Jessie had been planted and was growing with each passing day and I knew the One who was cultivating it. Our wedding photo still hung on a side wall in our living room and had been overlooked ever since the day it was hung—so had Jessie. I stood in front of it and took in the image as if for the first time. We stood together smiling as bride and groom with a Mexican beach in the background. We were so young, completely absorbed in our own selfish pursuits and drowning in our own secret pain. We had no love to give. The truth is we had none for ourselves either.

"Jesus, tell me it's not too late," I whispered under my breath, standing before the photo. "Wherever she is, surround her in your love and heal what's broken inside." A pause. "And please let me see her again."

I unpacked what little there was to return to my closet and dresser and stood under a warm shower for longer than usual, collecting my thoughts in the cloud of steam. It was Tuesday. I would officially return to the concert hall next week and my orchestra was planning what they called 'A Celebration of Life' party in my honor this coming Friday. Their clever irony in their use of the phrase had not been lost on me. I had come so close to death, but in the process encountered a new way of living I could have never imagined for myself. Joy had moved in and I could honestly say that life, for the first time, was something worth celebrating.

That evening, after a quick sortie to gather the basic grocery items and replenish the fridge, I settled down in front of blank sheets of music paper and a hot cup of tea. The heavenly music, which had not so long ago enveloped me like a symphonic waterfall, now taunted me beyond the distant veil of eternity eluding my creative grasp. I sat in front of the blank sheets for a time with my eyes closed and my ears straining for a clear note to start with—but no note came. As I had suspected while absorbing the celestial sounds from heaven, its music could never be captured in the simplistic melodies of mortals.

With my eyes still closed, the faces of those the Father had shown me while I was with him emerged in my imagination. Travis Bishop. Alfie. Jessie. Conviction began to stir in my heart in the form of a thought. What if I was never intended to replicate the melodies and songs I heard? The Father had never handed me a key to unlock their mystery. Instead, he had shown me people making music of their own, which flowed from their hearts—hearts which had been fused with his. Granted, they were not all musicians, at least my wife wasn't, and of that I could be certain. But somehow I knew they would all play a part in the music I was now meant to write. And I knew which one I would start with in the morning.

Chapter 25: A Beautiful Exchange

Over the bustling din, where Broadway and Columbus Avenue intersected, I could hear the familiar tune from one of its more routine musicians getting louder as I neared the corner at West Sixty-fifth. Alfie was still there. He wore the same loose-fitting Yankees ball cap and wind breaker. Not much had changed — except for the man who now approached him.

"Hello Alfie," I said, coming to a stop before his open case.

"Well now, bless me real good, if it isn't Mr. Mann. Ha ha." Alfie continued to pick naturally at his strings while he spoke with a radiating smile. "I heard about you being in the hospital. I've been reading the stories in the paper. I've been praying for you, Mr. Mann, and I can't tell you how good it is to see you this fine morning."

I smiled back with a knowing grin. "It's really good to see you too Alfie — more than you know." I said, reaching my hand into my left pocket. "In fact it's you that I'm coming to see this morning. I've been thinking about you and… I figure it's only right, since I've been away for so long…" I pulled what I was reaching for out of my pocket and let the one hundred dollar bill drop into his open case. "…that you accept this as back payment for all the days I've missed." My grin turned to a smile and I had to fight back the tenant reservoir of emotion which, these days, constantly threatened my composure.

His strumming stopped. Alfie gazed upon the bill with a gaping mouth, his face awash with an expression of disbelief.

"Well now, Mr. Mann... I don't..." His voice drifted as he searched for words, but only a pause followed before he looked up at me again.

"Thank you," he said staggeringly. "Thank you so much."

I knelt down in a crouch to meet his face at the same level. "Of course, Alfie. You're welcome," I said. "You know, I've always been quite an admirer of your music." I shifted slightly to get more comfortable on the ground and reached into my right pocket. "In fact, I have something I'd like to ask you."

"Sure, Mr. Mann. Sure," he replied.

"And please, call me Michael."

"Right. Uh—Michael it is." My name came reflectively from his still bewildered and measured voice.

"I'm hoping you can help me with my next composition," I said, now pulling out six more hundred dollar bills from my right coat pocket and holding them out to Alfie. "I know what I'm asking would take you away from your work here for a while so I'd also like to pay you for your time. This is just an advance and more or less what a musician would receive when playing with me in the Philharmonic."

Alfie remained as still as a rabbit under the glare of a hunting eagle for some time while his own eyes studied my face in wondering and wide-eyed examination. He searched for any indication he might have somehow stumbled out of reality for a moment, into a dream which would evaporate the next time he blinked.

"Mr. Mann I... I don't know what to say. Surely, I don't," Alfie managed with a hint of cracking in his voice.

"Alfie. Your music has a substance that so much of our best

music in this world lacks but so desperately needs." My words came out bolstered with conviction. "It's love, Alfie. Your music is saturated with a love that spills out of you in every note." Leaning in closer, I placed the additional bills inside his case. "Would you do me the honor of sharing your music with my orchestra and with me?" I asked. My eyes finally hazed over with moisture blurring my vision of his inquisitive gaze.

Alfie's expression shifted as though he found what he had been searching for. His open- mouthed daze transitioned into a knowing smile as he nodded his head with a subtle bob.

"Well now Michael... I do believe you've met him — haven't you? My God, yes. I do believe you have." He burst out in jovial laughter and clapped his hands together contentedly. "Sweet Jesus. Thank you, Jesus! Ha ha! My, if this isn't the most wonderful thing." He exclaimed.

It was now my turn to be shocked. "How do you know this?" I asked.

"Well now. I've been praying all this time for you. Every day you would walk on by I would pray that God would lift them heavy burdens off your heart. Whatever they were they was riding you like a sack of bricks! It wasn't all that hard to see. But now Michael... now those sacks are gone and only one person in the whole world who can take a load off like that," Alfie said with a wink.

"Alfie, my friend. I think we've got a lot to talk about," I said. I stood and dried my eyes with a sleeve. "Would you come with me today? My office isn't far from here." I smiled, stretching out my hand in a gesture to follow.

Alfie slowly placed his worn out guitar inside the battered case and closed its straps with a snap, snap. He stood with labored exertion, holding his guitar case in the other hand.

"Lead the way, Michael. I'd be most happy to. Lead the way."

As we crossed the street in the direction of David Geffen Hall, Alfie asked a question.

"Six hundred dollars. My God. That what you folks make in a week?"

I laughed. "No, Alfie. That's what we make in a day."

Jessie lay on Samantha's couch curled up in a ball. She stared blankly through the T.V. screen as scenes from a mid-day soap flickered on low volume. Samantha's apartment had been home for the past weeks and a growing collection of empty wine bottles now added to her bundle of suitcases still stacked and hardly opened in the corner of the living room. Sam was not bothered by the sprawl from her guest. She was rarely in her own home most of the time. She taught yoga classes during the day at the gym where they worked together, and enjoyed a lavish night life, sharing beds with a handful of men from around the city in the evenings. Whenever Sam was home, conversation was shallow and brief, often accompanied by multiple bottles of sweet wine, some hors d'oeuvres, and a sappy Rom-Com.

"Just leave him, Jess. I don't understand what you're so tormented over. There are plenty of other rich men in the city and you've got miles left to go with that cute ass of yours. Might as well use it while you've got it." Sam would say dividing her attention loosely between her phone and T.V., while sipping back generous portions of wine.

"Hm," Jess would offer in response, non-committedly, while her thoughts drifted to her last conversation with Michael.

'I know you're having an affair...'

Being exposed with the simple statement both unsettled and freed her. How did he find out? How long had he known? How much did he know? The questions hammered her thoughts in rapid succession while simultaneously releasing her from a weight she didn't realize she carried. He knew. She could now leave him like she had planned. It was over.

Or was it?

'I'm sorry for never showing you the love you deserve...'

'God is good...'

'He'll never leave you... and neither will I.'

What the hell had happened to her husband? She had always imagined what his next words might be if he ever confronted her about the affair. A squall of profanity. Objects thrown. Shattered glass followed by a quick exit with no reason to ever return. Not exactly what one would call a clean or amicable break, but he was supposed to want her out as badly as she would want to leave. It should have been easy. But she never anticipated the words she heard. Their incessant refrain echoing in her mind battered her heart like breakers on a sediment cliff's edge. She was crumbling and didn't know why.

Compounding her affliction was the mention of God. It hit her like a hammer strike on glowing metal. Her fury was liberated and her pain rose up all around her in the form of shadows from her past, threatening to swallow her in darkness forever.

Where was God when she... she dared not continue with even the thought. It was too painful.

God had left her a long time ago. She was sure of that. And if he was so good why would he let that monster... She was only six years old, for God's sake.

No. If there was nothing to love about her then...

She was doing Michael a favor by leaving. Surely he would figure that out eventually. Leaving her was supposed to be as effortless as leaving trash on the curb.

But the string of texts kept piling up on her phone.

Sunday: *"Remember the time we danced on the beach in Mexico? I'll never hold a treasure more valuable than you. I love you."*

Monday: *"I don't know why I'm still alive, but I can't imagine going through the rest of my life without you. I love you."*

Tuesday: *"I'll be home soon. I hope to see you there. There's so much more to say and I just want to talk. In the meantime, know that I love you no matter what."*

In sharp contrast to Michael's vulnerable and relentless pursuit of her heart, Carl, who had been her lover over the past number of months, had sent her a few texts of his own: *"Hey baby, when am I going to see u next? Can't stop thinking about our last time and that hot, sweaty body of yours."* Carl's texts used to thrill her with an intoxicating excitement when they came but now, they felt like invitations onto the deck of a sinking ship. For now, all of her texts were going unanswered. She had nothing left to say.

Alfie and I approached one of the side doors of the Hall and I used my key card to swipe us in. *Still works*, I thought to myself. We entered and the door closed behind us with a clack, which reverberated through a hallway of vaulted ceilings and marble floors. To my relief, no one had seen us come in. I wanted this time with Alfie to go uninterrupted. I had been waiting for this moment for a while and there was a lot to discuss.

"Just one sec, Alfie" I said, looking down at my phone. "I've just got to do one quick thing."

Alfie could have waited in that one spot for hours. He stood mesmerized, absorbing the magnitude of his surroundings. Though the iconic structure towered before him from just across his street corner for years, he'd never thought the day would come when he would stand inside its walls.

I wrote another text to Jessie and pressed send with a silent prayer under my breath.

"You're loved and held in the Father's embrace and you will always be welcome in mine. I love you."

"Okay Alfie, ready to go," I said turning my focus back to him. Looking up from my phone, I noticed his fixed fascination and thought it best not to rush the moment. These halls had become common to me, but even I had to appreciate the significance of where I stood.

"Impressive, isn't it?" I asked.

"Yes, it sure is," Alfie said in hushed wonder.

"You should see the main hall. Come on. Follow me."

We walked through some of the back rooms and corridors where the orchestra would practice and assemble. In one of the hallways we crossed paths with a security guard whose attention was immediately drawn to Alfie. He was about to say something when I quickly interjected.

"Hello James," I said casually.

I was most likely unrecognizable dressed in my more comfortable clothes and runners while appearing more gaunt and pale than I had ever been. The guard had to take a second look before realizing in a jolt of revelation who had addressed him.

"Mr. Mann!" James exclaimed in surprise. "I wasn't expecting to see you back here for another week."

I put a finger to my mouth mimicking a mock hush. "I'm trying to keep a low profile to get re-acquainted with the place before the real work begins again."

"Of course," James replied.

"Good to see you again, James." I said, now resuming my walk. Alfie followed, giving James a polite smile and nod which was now met with a gracious return of the same.

"You too, Mr. Mann. Take care!" James said.

The padded footfalls on the stage from our soft-soled shoes carried across the grand hall with magnified reverberations accentuating the impressive acoustics surrounding us on all sides. Some of the more implacable critics of the hall over the years maintained its overall size was too large compared to the more intimate concert halls constructed in the last two decades. The sound evaporated in the open space of the vaulted ceilings and the stage felt too far away for those seated along the back balcony rows. I had heard it all many times before. Indeed, the hall's simple architecture was more pragmatic than some of the more elegant or modern concert halls tucked deep inside the cultural capitals of the world. But still, in the silence, the sound of a pin dropping on the stage could be thrown to the far wall and back with ease, and a violin solo in the sacred space could break your heart.

Alfie stood on the stage for a time as though lost in a dream. He stood motionless, possibly too afraid the slightest movement might stir him awake and he might find himself back on the street corner or in his small cot in the basement of the church. His tattered guitar case and grubby clothes stood out in sharp contrast against the backdrop of the expensive wood paneling surrounding the stage projecting a glowing amber sheen. The minimum standard of dress for performers who played here was formal evening attire. I was certain Alfie had never owned or even worn such dress, but none of that mattered. Alfie had a sound of pure gold to share with the world and I was going to make that happen.

So much had changed for me since I last stood on this stage, I contemplated. The last time I had stood here, I had collapsed and was carried away by ambulance while clinging to life by a wisp of thin air. My trajectory then, as a celebrated composer, was my only path in life; that trajectory now resonated like a toneless and empty noise. After hearing the matchless transcendence of heaven's song I was now bound to the heart of its source. My path was now a pursuit of that heart and sound alone and the results would just be a byproduct. I saw my elevated status as a set of shoulders musicians like Alfie could stand on.

A subtle vibration from my phone in my pocket broke me from my trance. An electrical current of anticipation shot through me at the thought of Jessie responding to my messages. Pulling my phone out, and cradling it with two hands as though I held a fragile heirloom, I looked at the message and my shoulders slumped in dejection. It was my mom checking in to see how I was doing—not Jessie as I had hoped. I tapped out a quick reply, grateful to have such nurturing in my life and pocketed my phone again.

"Come on, Alfie. Let me take you into my office. I'd like to show you something else and you will finally be able to put your guitar down."

The sound of my voice shook Alfie from his fixed gaze and he turned to face me with a smile.

"Well, alright then, but it can't be anything near spectacular as this, and that's the truth."

We'll see about that, I thought to myself, as we both turned back towards the stage door, leaving another sound of footfalls to echo through the great hall.

We came to my office encountering no one else in the halls and stepped inside. The first thing to catch most people's eye was the back wall behind my desk which faced them as they entered. This was intentional. I facetiously called it my bragging wall and feigned indifference to it whenever I welcomed guests in while in truth, I basked in the presence of my accolades sometimes to the point of being more cognizant of the bravado behind me than my guests themselves. A low row of shelves held the awards and trophies, spoils from my short-lived history lined wall to wall like imposing sentinels standing in formation behind their sovereign. Above was a smattering of framed photos — dignitaries posing with me interspersed with a healthy balance of my profile plastered across the covers of magazines such as *People*, *Time*, and *Rolling Stone*.

But Alfie didn't notice the wall as he walked in. He scanned the room quickly taking in his surroundings until his eye fell on a long-neglected photo framed and sitting on the corner of my desk. It was the same photo of Jessie and I on the beach sealed with an invisible layer of dust. Instinctively, he picked it up and stared for a quiet moment.

"Is this your wife?" he asked in a tone of gentle reverence.

"I hope so," I replied.

"Mm," Alfie hummed with a subtle nod of his head—almost knowingly, despite the complicated response I had provided.

"She's mighty pretty." He handed me the frame. Taking it, I sat on the corner of my desk while Alfie sat down across from me.

With my sleeve, I wiped the film of dust off the glass and stared at our photo again.

"Yes she is," I said suddenly filled with the urge to wipe every last object of distinction from my back wall like an upturned table being cleared in a righteous rage. I would trade it all in a second if I could have that moment on the beach again. This photo was the only thing now worth hanging on my wall.

I placed the frame back on my desk and turned my attention back to Alfie, unsure of what to say next.

"Were you ever married, Alfie?"

Alfie's eyes glazed over in distant remembrance and he was silent for a while. Then he spoke. "Mary was the most beautiful girl I ever did know," he said wistfully. He was still smiling, though his eyes spoke of a deep sorrow.

"We were just kids when we married." He chuckled softly with a slight shake of his head. His smile caused him to squint, causing more lines to appear below the rim of his ball cap on the furrowed dark skin of his brow. There were most likely more signs of age buried beneath the peppered grey stubble outlining the rest of his face, its muted tones highlighting the glow of his teeth when they showed. Then his expression changed.

"But she died giving birth to my baby girl," he said still shaking his head. "That was a sad day." And then he was silent. He didn't need to explain.

"I'm sorry, Alfie," I said sincerely. "I can't imagine how hard that must have been for you."

His head became still and he tilted it in my direction, but stared off in the distance as though looking at someone. "But now I've got two angels in heaven, and they're watching over me. Their smiles both as bright as the sun does shine." He fixed his eyes back on mine. "I'll be with them again one day. I know it. But I'm grateful for every day I get down here. This life is the most precious gift that God does give."

He spoke as confidently as if he stood in heaven in that moment staring in the eyes of his wife and daughter. Did he already know? Had God somehow shown him the same things I had seen? It very well could have been, but I let the thought go as I wasn't ready to venture there yet myself.

"Have you ever been angry at God?" I said, my eyes searching expectantly for an expression on his face to tell more than words ever could. But his eyes conveyed a peace which reinforced the integrity of his words that followed.

"No," he said without hesitation. "No, I can't say as I have been angry at God. Now don't misunderstand. In my life there has been more…" His voice quavered and trailed off. He looked at the ceiling as if holding back tears that might spill out if his face were tilted towards the ground. He stared up for a second then recovered quickly. He started to speak again in an impassioned whisper, locking his eyes with mine.

"I have seen more ugliness in a world that's near forgotten what it's like to be human. I have stood at the graves of them whose time has come too soon; mothers burying their children and all their hope with them. I have known the raw grip of sorrow on my soul and walked through the valley of the shadows." A single tear welled and streamed from his unblinking eyes as they remained

fixed on me. "And I have been angry, yes. Lord I have been angry —
but I have *never* been angry at God... Never." His voice trembled
slightly as he said the last never. "It was God that put me together
when I was but broken all to pieces. It was God that met me in my
valley of shadows. He was the One who came looking for me when
I was so lost and he asked me for something then." He paused long
enough for me to fill the silence.

"What?"

"An exchange," he said.

His words rang out with an echo of those spoken to me in
eternity. I struggled to maintain repose as my heart pulsated in my
constricting throat as I heard them repeated by this extraordinary
man.

"He gave me joy when I told him he could have my sorrow.
When I had enough of my own ugly thoughts, he took them and
gave me a wonderful, wonderful peace. And when the weight of
my anger became too much for me to carry, he took it away — it took
me a time to figure out all I had to do was ask. In exchange for that,
I got me a new heart and it was filled with love. Love, Mr. Mann,
like I never thought there could be in all this wide world." Alfie
cleared his throat. "So to answer your question Mr... uh,
Michael..." he said. "To answer your question, I have never pointed
my anger *at* God. I've let it fall at His feet."

I stared at him. "Alfie, I wish I'd met you a long time ago."

With a delicate chuckle he replied, "Well, this time or some time
ago, it doesn't much matter. We'll all figure sometime or another
that God won't ever stop chasing us down. Never! And that's the
truth."

The first wave of emotion was receding and we gently rode its ebb down between the valley of the swells. I was nodding my head in agreement. "Will you come with me?" I asked. I stood up from the corner of my desk indicating another door to my right. Alfie had settled back into his easy-going demeanor and stood up to follow.

"Bring your guitar," I said. And Alfie picked up his guitar case.

The next room over was similar in size to my office, but obviously used for a different purpose. Along the length of the wall facing us was another display. Hanging from end to end was a wide array of instruments used in our concert orchestra from the piccolo to the piano. Every section was represented in the great collection: woodwinds, strings, brass, and percussion. At the far end of the room, along the back wall, was an upright honey oak Steinway piano. There was also a German-made concert cello with a rosewood sheen which refracted the light bouncing off the shiny surfaces of the instrument wall. I could play each one with expert proficiency, but my favorite had always been the violin.

There were four violins hanging at the end of the wall, each one a different make offering distinct tones discernible only to a well-trained ear. Next to the violins were two guitars. One a classical guitar with a red cedar soundboard and rosewood body, and the other a custom-made Martin acoustic. I removed the acoustic guitar from its place on the wall and gently ran my thumb over its strings giving off a muted hint of sound. I then made quick work of picking individual strings from top to bottom tuning each one as I went. Satisfied with my single pass, I strummed through a simple chord progression with more vitality and a pulse of rich melodic tones resonated from the heart of the guitar masterfully encased in sitka spruce and Macassar ebony. The sound always brought a smile to my face.

"Would you like to give it a try?" I asked Alfie casually.

"Well now, that is one mighty fine guitar. I can't say as I've ever heard such a beautiful sound from an instrument before," Alfie said with obvious enchantment.

"Grab one of those stools over there. Put your case down and take a seat," I said.

Alfie sat and I handed him the guitar. He took it from my hands as delicately as a new father cradling his first newborn child and held it for a while, taking in its feel and weight. His eyes travelled along the nouveau vine inlay running down the length of the ebony fretboard and his fingers gently followed along the strings until they were placed in position. He closed his eyes and began to pick deftly on the metal strings. He began to fill the instrument room with a sound it had never before been witness to in all the years of playing host to some of the best musical talent in the world.

We let the moment linger like a meditation, where the awareness of the body is all that matters as the chest rises and falls with no commitment to time. The consonance between the beat of his heart and the cadence of his tune could be felt in palpable waves of repose as he played. I closed my eyes and let the sound filter through me like the photosynthesis of a mountain flower. In my imagination, I could see the image of two glowing figures: a mother and daughter, their robes of white a stark contrast against their dark skin that radiated like amethyst and sapphire. A great tree rose like a column of steam from the mouth of a thermal spring in the background. Alfie's music was transcendent.

The song came to an end too soon. I could have listened for hours without tiring.

"That was simply beautiful," I said. My words felt inadequate.

"My, my, Michael. That is high praise coming from the likes of you. Thank you." Alfie's eyes glimmered with joie de vivre as rare as a golden pearl.

"That just makes this exchange that much more compelling," I said, now allowing my concealed excitement to show.

"Exchange?" Alfie asked.

"It's nothing like the one you described to me. Nothing like the one I've encountered myself, but one nonetheless that puts a smile on God's face and I hope on yours too."

Alfie's eyes widened with an expression that told me he anticipated what I would say next.

"I would like to exchange my guitar for yours," I said, reaching down for Alfie's beat up old case and opening the clasps with a click, click. I picked up his tired and worn out guitar and regarded it with a genuine look of admiration. If only this instrument could talk; the stories it could tell, I thought. My eyes met his and my brow raised slightly as if to ask, 'what do you say?'

Alfie's eyes widened further until they were two large white spheres enveloped in the mantle of his dark-lined skin. He had searched my expression for a hint of hesitation and found none. He had known disappointment from others who had started with good intentions and never followed through. This, he told himself, was actually happening.

"I ... I don't..." His voice shook with a tremor and he gazed down at the guitar in his hands. When he looked up again his eyes held fresh tears suspended in glossy sheens of moisture ready to spill over. His words came in labored intervals. "I haven't asked for much for myself since my Mary died," he started. "Anything I've ever really wanted in this life was a family. When they were gone, I had to believe that God had another plan." His eyes stared off into his distant past. "The Lord is my Shepherd, I shall not want..." He lingered in a reminiscent posture like one watching a lifetime go by.

"But lately..." His face brightened with a grin forming on one side of his mouth. "When I'm alone at night praying, I've got to thinking, how it might be nice to one day get me a new guitar. Mine is almost as old and tired as me." He chuckled. "I've been afraid that one day soon it might not be able to pull the strings tight no more, and then how would I-"

"Raise money for the people who no one sees?" The words were involuntary as I finished his sentence and a surprised look crossed both our faces.

"How did you...?" Alfie asked incredulously.

With those words I was committed to the course the conversation would now take, though I was unsure of where it might come to rest. "You can learn a lot when you die," I said with a smile. "And I learned that God sees what most of us can't. And you know what Alfie?" I asked determined to go for it.

"What's that now?" he said.

"He's been paying particular attention to you."

"Is that so?" he said more to himself than to me.

"Mary. Was that your wife's name?" I asked not to change the subject but to answer the question.

"Yes. Mary Willows was the prettiest girl I ever did see. On the first day we met I said to myself, 'I'm gonna marry that girl.' It took some time and convincing, but she eventually came around. And my, my, the pursuit was half the fun," he said with a twinkle in his eye.

"And you said you had a daughter?" I ventured.

His expression changed again and a recoil of sadness appeared on his face. "I did."

"What was her name?" I asked, sensitive to the fact I was now treading between the cracks of a broken heart.

"Her name is Gracie. Our little Gracie. She died on the same day with her mama. During labor something went wrong and I lost them both. My Gracie would be thirty-four this year," he said in a whisper. "I might even have had me some grandbabies by now, but I try not to pay too much mind to those thoughts."

The conversation had taken on a life of its own and I realized I had no more questions at that point. I felt the time had come to let Alfie into the excerpt of my journey which would link the two of our lives in an intimate and profound way.

"Alfie, this is going to sound absurd," I started. "When I was in my coma, I wasn't just lost in a dark void or an unconscious vegetative state. In fact, there was no darkness at all. He was there."

Alfie's look and slight nod of the head told me he understood and was not going to dismiss what I had to say. I pressed on.

"The narrative of a person's life is a veiled mystery to the rest of us who only witness what lies on the surface. None of us can say that we truly know another individual. Most of us cannot even say we truly know ourselves. Why he chose to show me the people and lives he did, I'll never fully understand. But I sure am grateful that he did."

That came off too philosophical, I thought. What was it I was trying to say? Still holding Alfie's old guitar, to buy some time and process my thoughts, I stood up from the stool I had been resting on and walked over to the display wall and hung his where the Martin guitar had rested all those years. Alfie's guitar looked like a battle-worn soldier, bloodied and fatigued, standing in a column of fresh infantrymen who had yet to see a front line. I turned from the case and faced Alfie again.

"Alfie, what I'm trying to say is... your wife and daughter... I saw them."

A fresh sheen of moisture materialized in his unblinking and awestruck stare before cresting in a thin stream down the side of his face. His lower jaw moved with a subtle quiver.

"For some reason, God decided to let me into a small window of your life when I was in my coma," I said. "He showed me that your life here is beautiful and carries more impact than a whole city full of churches ever have. And when I was in heaven—at least, I think that's where I was—he showed me your wife and your daughter. They're so beautiful—the very grace and pride of heaven."

"You saw my girls?" he asked with a trembling whisper. "You saw my Gracie?"

"Yes," I said.

"What did my little girl look like?"

"Alfie, she's still your little girl. It doesn't look like she's aged much past ten there. Your wife was braiding flowers in her hair." And then, with a flash of spontaneous insight I added, "I think she might be waiting for you and doesn't want to grow up until you get a chance to hold her as the little girl you've always imagined she might have been."

Alfie burst into convulsing sobs which doubled him over on the stool where he sat. Half afraid he would crush the guitar still resting in his hold and half afraid he would fall off the stool, I took the guitar from his lap and placed it gently on the floor, then shouldered his face as I leaned in to put my arms around him. He

216

crumpled into me and we both fell to the floor in a controlled drop like an imploded building, and came to rest in an embrace on our knees. Alfie buried his face in my chest and wept out loud like a little boy in the throes of unabashed grief in the healing waves of release I had known while in the arms of my father in heaven. As emotion took us both and the sound of our cries filled the little room, for just a moment, I thought I could hear the music of heaven once again.

Chapter 26: The Sterling

Alfie looked good in his new clothes. Today it was a simple pine-green buttoned shirt, new navy-blue jeans with a brown belt, and matching brown leather shoes. It took some convincing to bring him to this point of acceptance and comfort in his new wardrobe, but I insisted. Not to mention the support I gained from his friends when we discussed it in the church's soup kitchen the first time I paid them a visit. That tipped the scales in my favor. It had been a few weeks already since our encounter in my office at David Geffen Hall. From that time on, we had been together every day writing and playing music together and getting better acquainted.

On one evening last week, when Alfie was about to depart for his regular evening rounds, I asked if I could come along. I wanted to experience in real life what had, until now, been something more out of a dream.

"That's alright, Mr. Mann," Alfie had said. "But you gonna stand out like a canary in a cat convention." And he bellowed in delightful laughter.

In a reversal of roles, Alfie's fashion advice to me was to dress down as best as I could for the tour that evening. But even in my old Reebok hoodie and some blue jeans, it was clear that I hailed from a different part of the city. I gained so much from the tour that any discomfort I felt seemed insignificant. I met with some of Alfie's longtime friends, most of whom were humble enough to receive from Alfie and too poor to ever repay his kindness. Some of them I remembered from the night I walked the same streets and corridors with the Father, others were new and beautiful faces.

The highlight of the evening was meeting Gloria and the three beautiful kids, Tyrell, Oscar, and Talliah. It warmed my heart feeling the overwhelming measure of their love in the midst of such poor living conditions. I determined that night to find a more comfortable place this family could one day call home.

But tonight it was Alfie's turn to tour with me and our sortie called for contemporary attire. The pub was an upscale bar in Lower Manhattan called The Sterling. A small sign fastened to the red brick on the side of the heritage low rise building read, 'Live Music Tonight – Featuring Blake Fender.' I made reservations for eight o' clock with the knowledge that we would most likely stay until the closing hours in the early morning. Alfie and I had both become accustomed to being creatures of the night and operated on limited hours of sleep.

The black leather and mahogany of the booths in the bar reflected the glow of the dim lighting with a dull phosphorescent sheen creating an atmosphere where patrons could easily vanish into obscurity while enjoying fusion cuisine and New York's indie music scene. The only real light in the place was focused on the small stage in one corner where Blake Fender was deftly plucking out his own rendition of a Bob Dylan tune on his guitar, while also playing a harmonica suspended on a rack around his neck. We found our seats and ordered samosas and soda waters. I told Alfie we were going to meet my friend Kyle, known to everyone else in the room that evening as Blake Fender.

The evening was about more than just introductions. Since my awakening, my thoughts had been consumed with a new kind of music—music which I knew wasn't meant to be played in the same design I had always known. I also knew I was not meant to write it alone.

Kyle's set finished and he joined us at our booth as the canned ambient house music played lightly over the sound system.

"You sounded great up there," I said standing up to greet him with a hug. "I'd like you to meet a dear friend of mine." Turning to Alfie I said, "Alfie, this is Kyle Thornton, another one of New York's best kept musical secrets," I said cordially as Kyle sat down.

"Very glad to meet you. Very glad," Alfie said reaching his hand across the table for a shake.

"The pleasure is all mine, Alfie. Michael has told me about you. You're not so bad on the guitar yourself I hear," Kyle said.

"Oh, I do get on I guess," Alfie responded with a dismissive chuckle.

The two talked for a while as I sat back and listened. The samosas arrived to our table where they remained untouched. We didn't come together for the food. When conversation settled into a natural lull, I started in.

"Kyle, you remember that day at the hospital when you and Kate came back to visit?"

"I do," Kyle said reflectively.

"How is Kate doing by the way?" I asked.

Kyle's face lit up with a wistful smile and both Alfie and I recognized the look of young love breaking out across his face. He beamed as he spoke. "She's doing well. She and I, uh… well, we see a lot of each other these days," he said with a goofy grin.

"I'm glad to hear it. Kate is a great girl. Beautiful too," I said.

"Mm-hm," Kyle managed to mumble still smiling.

"Sorry, Kyle. That's not what I came to talk about," I winked as I said it. "That day in the hospital—I said that you and I should write music one day together. I'm here to ask you if you'd like to play with me in my next concert."

The goofy grin was gone, replaced instantly with wide eyes and an awestruck stare as though I had offered him the lost treasure of Atlantis.

"Are you being serious right now?" Kyle asked. He glanced at Alfie who sat in quiet assurance gesturing a knowing nod. He looked back at me, searching my face with wild-eyed hope the words he heard were true—and not too good to be true.

"Have you ever heard the expression beauty from ashes?" I asked.

"Of course I have," Kyle said without breaking his gaze.

"I've spent my life running from the fires of life—as if we can really escape them. I've tried to put as much distance between myself and the ash piles as I could and then raged at God with accusations of abandonment." With a strained whisper, I continued. "But he was with me the whole time. In the fires all along and waiting for me in the ashes with a gift. An exchange. The beauty of new life that always follows the flames. I thought I had to make it on my own and never returned to the place of my pain. Most of us don't. But there in the ashes is reserved the deepest places of the heart and oddly enough, the only place we truly find healing." I paused to take some sips from my water and glanced around the dimly lit lounge. People were leaning in over their tables engaged in muted conversation. Returning my attention back to Kyle, I saw he had not broken his gaze and was waiting for me to continue.

"It has been the same with music. Music is everything to me. It's been my whole life. But I've done it on my own using it like a cave I could disappear into when all along it was meant to be an expression from the deepest places of my heart. A place I've been too afraid to go."

For the first time Kyle looked away to check his watch. He was probably expected to return to the stage shortly.

"But you've both been there and the music you play carries an expression of depth and beauty I want on my stage. When music comes from that place, it eclipses sound and measure and brings to life the things that were dead." And then I added with a chuckle, "I should know — I've experienced it myself."

Alfie was nodding his head in agreement and a smile.

"Will you help me?" I asked looking back at Kyle.

Kyle hesitated, allowing all he had heard settle like the accumulation of snow on a windless day. He had played in venues of all kinds over the years and thought with contentment that the small stage at The Sterling ventured close to his ceiling. He didn't need his name in lights or a bigger stage but the hammering of his heart betrayed an excitement and desire for something he never would have dared to hope for. His thoughts went to Gramps Thornton. He imagined sitting with him in this moment and catching the look of pride coming across his face. Kyle had to bite his tongue to keep the tears back.

Finally Kyle replied, "It would be my honor."

Chapter 27: The East Baltimore Street Mission

Travis's feet were sore. He had been on them all day. A common complaint for most average adults working a harried afternoon with little time to rest. But for Travis, the added complication of having bad circulation in his legs and feet accentuated the discomfort. He was still in his twenties, but years spent on the streets chasing after his addictions and running from his pain had been cruel and hard on his body, making him look and feel older than he was. Some of the collapsed veins in his legs from the constant abuse to his body never fully healed. Some never came back at all. But the minor discomfort was not enough to slow his pace. He had been sober and healthy for two and a half years and his life was now dedicated to helping others get out of the same nightmare he knew all too well.

The East Baltimore Street Mission was located just a few blocks away from a park bench on South Central Ave. where Travis was found that frigid January night half frozen, but too stoned to notice. His feet and legs were bare and the unknown hours of exposure certainly compounded upon the long-term effects to his poor circulation. After his hospitalization, he was picked up by the same kind soul who had brought him there the week before and shepherded him back to the Mission. That was two and a half years ago and Travis was still there with no plans on leaving. He was among friends and family and his life was fueled with a passionate purpose.

His rescuer from that fateful evening was Eric, who had been with the Mission for over twenty years after his own recovery from a life of addiction. Eric became Travis's sponsor, mentor, and now a lifelong and trusted friend. Together, they were running the Mission with a team of some of the most beautiful and dedicated people the city of Baltimore would never know or hear about. They remained anonymous as their work went on tirelessly in the shadows.

The last group of residents had just piled through the kitchen and those who were lucky enough to have a bed that evening were settling in while the others dispersed back into the night. Travis was elbows deep in the wash sink, scrubbing away at one of the large soup pots used for most of the mission's daily meals when Eric stepped into the kitchen.

"Travis, there's someone here who'd like to see you. He says he knows you from some time ago," Eric said. "He's waiting in the dining hall."

Travis, his arms still deep in the water and without turning his head from the work said, "Ok, I'll be out in just a minute."

The dining hall was lined with three rows of long tables stretched from one end of the room to the other with an aisle cut down the middle where the old linoleum had been worn down like a goat path. A door opened out on each end of the aisle. One door led out to the small entrance corridor where people spending the night checked in before settling in to the overnight beds upstairs. The other door led to the kitchen and staff rooms; this was where Travis stood when he saw me.

I sat in the middle of the room at one of the tables holding a tepid coffee in a styrofoam cup as he came into view. An involuntary nausea, indicative of the ominous premonition I felt those long years ago, crept up on me and I had to recover quickly, reminding myself I had come a long way in shedding the pain of the past. Almost fifteen years ago, Travis Bishop stood in a school room doorway and filled its frame with his imposing figure, immobilizing me in terror. This time, however, it was Travis who stood motionless in wide-eyed transfixion. He stared at me as though he had come face to face with the Angel of Death himself. We were both still for a time as the memories of the past tore through us in vivid limbic recall. I could hear my violin shattering against the wall and the wail of agony hemorrhaging from my broken heart. By his expression, I could tell Travis stood captive to the memories in the moment too, yet to what end I did not know. Was he haunted by the past as I had been and did he now feel remorse for some of his actions? I was the first to break the silence.

"Hello Travis," I said standing to my feet.

There was a prolonged silence as he studied my demeanor searching for malice or contempt. But, finding none, the tension in his shoulders slackened with an outward and audible sigh. "It's you," he said finally in a labored whisper, still not moving from his spot in the doorway.

"You weren't an easy one to find, that's for sure. But you can't imagine my relief when I heard you were only hours away in Bal..." I was cut off suddenly by his voice undulating in the throes of overwhelming emotion.

"I'm so sorry! I'm so sorry!" He bellowed, covering his mouth with one hand and steadying himself in the doorway with another. I started towards him in slow deliberate steps assuring him as I approached.

"I'm not mad, Travis. Not anymore," I said getting nearer to the doorway where he half stood, half leaned. Tears had welled in his eyes and were rolling unchecked down the sides of his face as he continued in his remorseful refrain.

"I'm so sorry. I'm so sorry."

His sudden reaction to my appearance displayed a tender vulnerability like a tree laid bare in autumn which I had not been prepared to encounter. It unsteadied my composure and roused me to emulate his emotion which, these days, was not hard to do. Standing only an arm's length away I said, "I know — I know that I carried anger for a long time over what happened when we were just kids. But I also know that the anger isn't there anymore."

I let the tears come, blurring my vision as the truth in my own words washed over the two of us like the fresh air that follows a heavy rain.

"I know that you were afraid then, just as much as I was, and your anger was lashing out at an injustice you couldn't fight back against. I know what that's like too," I said.

Travis listened, quietly staring at the floor. Finally he spoke having regained command of his voice. "You came all this way. Why would you do that?" He asked bringing his eyes to mine.

The smile appearing in my expression betrayed the excitement I felt having anticipated this moment from the day I first started my search for Travis. "Well," I said, "I came to invite you to a concert."

Chapter 28: Central Park

Jessie regarded a pile of freshly fallen leaves from the Central Park bench where she sat as they floated delicately above the surface of weathered stone pavers in an invisible whirlpool of crisp autumn air. With the wane of twilight casting long shadows from the west, their aimless revolutions resembled dancers circling an evening fire, throwing their shadows a great distance until they blended into the surrounding darkness. As she watched, she couldn't help think how her life felt like one of those leaves, discarded, lifeless, and tossed indiscriminately about by unseen forces with a cold indifference.

How long had she had been walking through the park? She couldn't remember. She had left the apartment in a blur with no destination in mind when Samantha arrived with a new guy for the evening. Rather than play the third wheel, though she knew she would be welcome to stay and maybe even participate in the fun, her gnawing awareness of dejection repelled her from anyone who tried to get close like two pieces from a broken magnet.

She had relinquished her yoga classes to others and gone completely silent on all who attempted to talk to her, including her lover Carl, and most of all, Michael. The texts continued to come in from both. Sporadically from Carl, most likely when his appetite for lust rose to a crescendo with no one in close proximity with whom he could satiate himself. But from Michael, they continued to come daily, his words of affirmation and grace eroding her resistance like a steady stream of water cutting furrows through a bank of sand.

How could he still continue to pursue her after what she had done to him? Couldn't he see she was no good? No more valuable than a worthless condom which had served its purpose and been tossed away? Her own deep self-loathing had come out of hiding a long time ago. She had run out of masks and could no longer bear to meet her own reflection. She should just make it easy on everyone around her and end her miserable life.

Hot tears appeared at her thoughts of suicide. A reminder that warm blood still coursed through her veins and she had not yet passed entirely into a numbing resolve. What was she supposed to do?

"What the fuck am I supposed to do?!" Her sudden outburst cut through the silence in the park, her tears provoking a dormant rage which erupted like embers fanned into flame in a dry forest bed. Glancing quickly around to make sure she was alone, she yelled: "God!"

And then crumpled over on her bench before repeating in a whisper between heaving sobs, "God."

She cried then like she had always wanted to as a little girl, but had never allowed herself the liberty. Her release into grief was absolute. She could run no longer. There was nowhere left to hide. It had finally caught up to her as she sat on the lonely park bench.

"If you're real then where were you when that monster took me into the closet again and again? Where were you then?" She looked up at the sky as its transfiguration in fire, bronze, and vermilion lingered with the setting sun. Her disdainful glare at the canopy of cloud above blurred with a watershed of tears obscuring her vision. Her voice quavered in a labored moan as though her words themselves cut like the slash of a knife.

"If everything my husband told me is true why haven't I heard anything from you?" She looked around to ensure she was still alone and buried her face in her hands continuing to weep. Her sorrow spilled out like hot, infected discharge from a deep wound. "Why the hell won't you talk to me?" she whispered.

Two subtle pulses from Jessie's phone vibrated in her pocket startling her enough to break the paralysis of her anguish for a moment. She reached for the phone in her pocket and stared at the lambent screen. It was a text from Michael.

"Jessie, I love you."

Jessie froze with the phone in her hand, unaware she was holding her breath. The words rushed into the vacuum from her question still suspended in the air as though spoken by a heavenly voice. A shiver of warmth coursed through her body causing the fine hairs on her arms and neck to stand up against the autumn breeze. In her moment of vulnerability she felt loved, found, and enveloped in an unexpected embrace by a Father reunited with His lost child. It took her by surprise, but her unravelling had only just begun.

Her phone vibrated as another text appeared; her eyes remained fixed on the screen.

"Please come to the concert tonight. I've reserved a special spot just for you."

Michael had been telling Jessie about his concert now for weeks. She never had any intention of going as the uncertainty of what to do after it was over circled her like sharks in the water. But his final invitation landed within the widening breach of her heart's defenses and pulled at her with the force of a river's current. She was about to take her first step.

On an impulse, while her heart began to race wildly in her chest, she started to write a text:

"It's over. I don't want to see you anymore."

As she exhaled deeply, she pressed send and the message was on its way. It was going to Carl.

A rush of dizzying light-headedness would have sent her crashing to the ground had she not still been sitting on the bench. She steadied herself and focused on her breathing while the moment passed and she began to collect her thoughts. The concert hall was only a fifteen-minute walk from the park and with her running shoes she could…

Wait! Jess thought now, staring down at her running shoes. *I can't show up to an evening concert dressed like this! And I can't go back to the apartment now either. All the good shops are closed by now, not that I could even afford to…*

Another text vibrated in her hand. A nauseating sensation churned in her stomach at the thought it would be some venomous response from Carl. Jess held the phone face down against her leg while long seconds passed. She'd have to look sooner or later. Taking a deep breath, she raised the phone to meet her gaze and she couldn't believe what she read. It was another text from Michael.

"One more thing. If you do decide to come, there is a new evening gown waiting for you in a private dressing room. Love, Michael."

Another rush of nerves and adrenaline fluttered through her body causing her to reach once more for the arm of the bench while the sensation passed and her mind raced. *What is going on?* She thought to herself. *And what is happening to me?*

A couple strolled by her bench, lost in conversation. They passed by and to Jessie's relief, they paid her no notice. No doubt her face would have still been flushed, her eyes puffy and red from the tears. Thank God she wasn't wearing any makeup.

But despite her sweatpants and hoodie, swollen eyes, flushed face, and tattered hair, somewhere between the moments which had passed, she had found a new resolve—or a new resolve had found her, she wasn't sure which. She stood to her feet and began her walk in the direction of the concert hall.

***

It occurred to Jessie a few times as she walked that she had no idea how she was supposed to get in once she arrived at the hall— especially looking as disheveled as she was. Over the course of her marriage to Michael, she had only attended a dozen or so concerts and knew only a handful of people by name. Twice she stopped at an intersection and agonized over her next step. Should she just turn back? she wondered. Who would believe she was the conductor's wife? She wasn't sure she believed it either. Even Jessie hadn't referred to herself as "Mrs. Mann" for over a year. But whether by some invisible hand of providence or her lack of any other option, both times she continued towards the hall.

Concert goers had descended upon the venue in eloquent droves adorning the sidewalks around the hall in splashes of vibrant color. A steady procession of stretch limousines deposited men and women clothed in fine evening attire off at the front doors. The air pulsed in electrified anticipation for what was being acclaimed through mainstream and social media alike as the 'Miracle Concert.' It would be Michael's first public appearance in five months since his fateful collapse and decent into the chasm between life and death.

231

But on a large banner draped over the main entrance the true name of the evening's concert was written: 'Beauty From Ashes.'

How could anything beautiful rise from the ashes of her life, Jessie thought, keeping her eyes down as she walked through the crowd congregating in front of the hall. She clutched at her jacket holding the collar up close to her chin as though trying to keep the chill of her inner turmoil out. Her walking had become aimless once again, though she now circled her destination. What was she supposed to do now? The easiest thing, she thought, could be to just text Michael and tell him she was outside, but something within her still resisted reaching out. Why even now did she feel trapped, as though her own body was a prison confining her to isolation as she navigated her way through dense crowds of humanity?

As she walked and wrestled with her thoughts a voice broke through the din of Lincoln Square calling out her name like an apparition from another life.

"Mrs. Mann! Mrs. Mann!" the voice called.

Though it startled her, Jessie continued to walk as though it were the growl of a chained dog or the jeering from a group of intoxicated men. Did she hear it or just think it? she wondered. As though in response to her question the voice came again and it was getting closer.

"Mrs. Mann! Mrs. Mann!"

Jessie looked up this time and turned in the direction of the voice. A security guard with a familiar face was approaching at a brisk pace waving one had in the air. She had seen this man possibly only a handful of times back in the days when Michael would take her into the hall through the back entrance and yet he seemed to know exactly who she was. Jessie stood waiting as the guard closed the last few yards that separated them until he stood before her breathing heavily.

"Mrs. Mann, I'm James," he said in between deep breaths. "We weren't sure if you were going to come or not. I'm so glad we found you."

We? she thought, still regarding the man with a blank stare thinly veiling her surprise. James touched an earpiece attached to a coiled wire coming from within the back of his jacket and spoke into a small receiver. "I found her. We're just outside the Lincoln Square entrance. Coming around the back now." He turned his attention back to Jessie. "Mrs. Mann, would you please come with me? Mr. Mann has arranged a private space just for you where you can get yourself ready." James extended one hand out in front of him with a subtle bow as if to reveal some hidden path only they could see.

"Um, thank you," Jessie heard herself say before they began their walk towards the hall.

Once they were through the doors, James escorted Jessie to one of a dozen private dressing rooms lining the backstage hallways. James stopped at a door where Jessie's name had been scribed on paper in her husband's writing: 'Jessie Mann.' He opened the door releasing a floral aroma that spilled out into the hall and immediately enveloped Jessie's senses. Inside, floral arrangements sat upon every surface in the small room. They covered the floor like a botanical flood, save for a few walking pathways carved out between the blossoming oases.

As Jessie slowly entered, taking in the scene before her like someone who had stumbled into a vivid hallucination, James politely dismissed himself. "I hope you find everything to your liking, Mrs. Mann. Inside the wardrobe you'll find a selection of

233

evening gowns which have all been selected just for you. There is a table with food and beverage just to the side here and the vanity drawers should have everything you need in the way of cosmetics. Some of the backstage ladies will be in to check on you shortly and provide any help you may need. I hope you have a pleasant evening." He closed the door leaving Jessie alone in the room.

Less than an hour ago, she had been sitting on a lonely park bench consumed with despair. Now she found herself standing before the open doors of a wardrobe, deftly running the fabric of elegant evening gowns between her fingers while surrounded by the flourish of a floral sea in bloom. She once had dreams of being a princess as a little girl. They were her most treasured dreams of all, and this experience was ushering her closer to its reality than she had ever come. But this was no dream, she told herself. The tactile feel of the soft fabric and the aromatic fragrance in the air reinforced the reality of the moment.

She lifted one of the gowns out of the wardrobe and held it up to her, turning to face the mirror at the vanity in a single graceful motion. The gown was sapphire blue silk with crystal embellished trim. It had a single shoulder band on the right draped across an open back, and there was a high slit cut up the thigh. It was one of the most beautiful things Jessie had ever seen.

She was about to begin changing when her eye was drawn to something on the center of the vanity. It was a single red rose resting on top of a white envelope. Once again, her name in Michael's writing was scribed on the front. Still holding the gown across one arm, Jessie approached the vanity and picked up the envelope holding it in her hand. Something about it conveyed significance as though the message held the weight of destiny. *To open it was to welcome a new life,* she sensed. And this thought introduced a powerful dichotomy of both elation and fear. Part of her wanted to read it and part of her wanted to run.

Jessie jumped as a light knock on the door shook her from deep thought, startling her back into the moment.

"Mrs. Mann, my name is Debbie; I'm one of the backstage assistants. Is there anything I can help you with or get for you?"

"I'm fine, thank you," Jessie replied courteously.

"Okay. Just give me a shout if there is anything you need, dear. I won't be far away." Debbie's footsteps fell away from the door.

Whatever was in the envelope would wait. Jessie placed it back on the desk and began to get ready.

Chapter 29: The Concert

My footfalls on the stage as I approached the podium were completely masked with the sound of cheering and applause from a concert crowd typically more reserved in their acclaim. Their enthusiasm was justified, however, given the nature of my return. Many in the audience were there on the evening of my collapse and many believed, once reports of my condition began to circulate, that it was the last time I would ever appear before them.

I stood to face them and took my first bow on the spot where I had fallen, in what seemed a lifetime ago. *I will remember this moment forever*, I thought to myself. Time held its breath while the audience and I embraced like long-parted friends in an eruption of reverie never before heard within the confines of the great hall. It was enough to conquer me completely. Every last strain of composure abandoned itself to overwhelming emotion. As I stretched my hands out towards them in gratitude and welcome, every additional bow allowed a fresh tear to fall on the stage until more than a dozen drops lay in a scattered collection at my feet.

As the wave began to slowly subside, my eyes rose to a private box seat to my right—it was empty. My heart sank with the unrealized hope of seeing Jessie seated there. *The night is just beginning*, I told myself. *There's still time for her to find her way here. Please God, let her come.*

My attention turned to the front three rows of floor seating. On most concert nights, it was easy to spot where the money sat and it was often in these front few rows. In this geographical region of the hall floor, most evening wear would easily run within the thousands of dollars until, by the middle, there was a healthy mix of suits and gowns in the low thousands to the high hundreds. By the back row, it was more common to see attire ranging in the lower hundreds of dollars like the dividing class line in a zip code. But that wasn't the case on this night.

There in the front row, along with fifty of his Street Mission regular residents from Baltimore sat Travis Bishop. We looked at each other and shared a smile. It was so good to see each other. The rest of the men and women seated in his group were dressed in various arrangements of the best clothing combinations they could piece together from a thrift store. A few of the better established ones wore a suit jacket over a shirt and mismatched tie. It was a beautiful sight.

Sitting beside Travis was his mom, who radiated with the delight of pride. The years had added lines to her skin and a dusting of grey in her hair but she still held the virtue and strength of the younger woman I witnessed during my unearthly journey with the Father. Beside her, my mom sat beaming with the same replete joy. Though this was the first night they had met, the two connected with a natural ease like two old friends coming together after a long passage of time. This night was as poignant and momentous for them as it was for their sons.

I turned to face my orchestra and almost fell to pieces once more at the sight of so many moist eyes. Among these had been some of my longest standing friends over the course of my career. I learned how many of them had visited my bedside often while I lay in my coma. I'm sure most of them believed we would never stand on a stage together again. I bowed to them with outstretched arms and another tear managed to escape, wetting the stage at my feet.

Before the concert started, I was expected to say a few words. A recipe card with some scribbled notes hid in my back pocket in case I blanked out. I never had to use it.

"Welcome and thank you all for being here. I'm so grateful to be standing here before you all tonight." Another roar of applause rose to a crescendo and more moments passed before my voice could be heard again over the din.

"It is my hope this evening to share with you some of the lessons I've learned over the past number of months: enduring love, true friendship, and the miracle that takes place in a great exchange of grace, which is offered to all but embraced by few. It is the exchange of our ashes in this life—pain, hatred, isolation—with the beauty of our intended purpose: love, joy, and peace. It took a brush with death and a prolonged coma for me to figure this out," I paused allowing the audience to respond with a light chuckle. "But there are some who embrace these truths wholeheartedly and live them daily. I know some of these dear souls and it will be my privilege to introduce you to them up on stage with me in a short while." My eyes fell back on the front row to Travis and I gave him a nod before addressing the crowd once more.

"Some other wonderful people are here with us tonight who could write volumes on their encounters with love, friendship, and their exchanges of beauty for ashes. They've travelled a long way and are right here at the front. Would you please welcome some truly beautiful people, my friends from the East Baltimore Street Mission."

With youthful vigor the group stood to their feet and waved at the people all around who were welcoming them with applause. Travis and I exchanged a knowing look. Though our backgrounds and journeys differed like fire and water, the same collision with grace brought us to this place together. We were pursued by love. Though we ran from it most of our lives, it overtook us like a crashing wave and pulled us into an ocean teeming with an abundance of life.

When the front row was seated once again it was time to start. I glanced up. Still no sign of Jessie.

"We're going to play some old favorites along with a few new pieces making their debut this evening. Many may recall my very first orchestra piece called the Song of the Trees or *Chant Des Arbres*. We're going to begin tonight with a new piece never before played before an audience called *Chant Des Arbres Célestes*. It is my old symphony reborn—much like my life. I could never replicate the sounds or cadence of heaven while I'm still bound and limited by gravity. It is a sound so beautiful, our world could never comprehend it. But we are all granted glimpses of heaven in this life when we open our hearts up to love. I hope you enjoy it."

With the first gesture from my baton, vivid images from my journey in heaven coursed through my mind like a pulse through the heart of God. Though the music from the stage exuded a tangible serenity from the subtle drone of the cello, to the fluttering inflection of the woodwinds, the change in the atmosphere took place as the felt presence of God infused every note transfiguring the music into a transcendent expression of theology.

***

Jessie followed as Debbie escorted her to the third floor where the last empty seat in the hall remained reserved and unoccupied. Almost an hour had passed since the concert started and its muffled sounds permeated through heavy doors and walls into the lobbies and corridors beyond the great hall as they went. Jessie had taken her time getting dressed and presentable and then allowed long moments to pass, sitting in her little room in silence while her mind drifted like a low fog over a still pond. Everything around her felt like a fragile dream which could dissipate the moment she awoke. Debbie's gentle knock on the door had startled her. She did not wake up and the dream continued.

Jessie's stunning figure and radiant beauty was an arresting sight. To watch her walk by, you wouldn't realize you were holding your breath. Crystals lining the trim of her sapphire blue gown glimmered with every stream of light which fell across her path. Her blonde hair fell straight down and below her shoulders framing the natural untamed beauty displayed in the details of her face. A remnant of childlike innocence still hid deep below the surface of natant blue in her eyes. But no one noticed as she found her seat in the dim light of the hall while the music serenaded a captive audience. In her hands she held the envelope, still sealed with Michael's letter to her inside.

The flow of the concert rose and fell like the arc of daylight on a long summer day. Each arrangement felt like the warmth of warm rays against closed eyes or a cool breeze against glowing skin. But it was all no more than an extended fuse in a slow burn, masterfully arranged to ignite the final number like the fading flares of dawn cast into the sky in a fire of bronze and crimson.

The house lights dimmed and silence fell across the hall. The audience held their breath as though a single sound might disrupt the tangible anticipation of the moment like a misspoken word at vespers. A single spotlight fell upon the center of the stage where a lone musician sat on a stool cradling an acoustic guitar. No one in the crowd would have ever imagined the august figure before them had only months ago played for pennies on a street corner only a stone's throw away.

No one that is, except for three little children seated in the front row next to their grandmother in a brand new wheelchair. Tyrell, Oscar and Talliah were dressed in the finest new clothes they had ever seen; they felt like models in a magazine. Their grandmother Gloria had a radiant glow about her. Her health had improved dramatically since the day they moved into a small bungalow in a quiet neighborhood in Queens—their new home. Gloria swore she would pay me back one day, but the smiles from her and the children held more value to me than the small mortgage I inherited. And now their smiles radiated as bright as the spotlight directed at Alfie on the stage.

A few more long seconds passed before his first deft pulls on the metal strings gave off a beautiful melody, releasing a corporate shiver of goosebumps throughout the crowd. The sound was like the union of sadness and joy gathered together under a banner of peace. Its cadence broke your heart and healed it all in the same moment. The tune rose and fell like the chest of an infant in tranquil sleep and the audience watched in rapt captivity.

Alfie's song returned to the same refrain over and over, like a mother repeating the same phrase to comfort a child. In between each refrain he would launch into a journey of vibrant sound covering the fretboard with his dancing fingers from end to end. No one wanted it to stop.

I stood on my podium in silent obscurity, while Alfie commanded the stage with his beautiful solo performance. I returned my eyes once again to the top corner box seat and immediately felt my heart race with an accelerated pulse causing my head to spin and my legs to wilt. It took everything to steady myself once again to keep me from collapsing once again. There, seated in quiet repose was Jessie. Her beauty took my breath away. Our eyes met and I managed my best smile conveying all the love which had grown in me like a flourishing oak. She stared at first, with her uncertain eyes studying my own. I knew the moment would end soon as Alfie's solo was coming to a close; the orchestra was lifting their instruments in anticipation. I silently mouthed the words "I love you" and watched with overwhelming delight as the crack of a subtle smile broke across her face.

As my arms went up, the entire stage woke to life in a burst of incandescent light. As they came down with a forceful sweep, the charge was lit and the orchestra erupted in a revival of rhythm and euphony engaging the senses in a rush of adrenaline. The wave of sound that flooded the hall carried a life of its own, in a style of music unexpected in such a setting. It became clear right away that the orchestra was now just an accompaniment supporting the melody coming from Blake Fender and his band who now appeared under bright stage lights.

The surge of electric guitar, bass, and drums introduced a vibrancy to the music like a sun shower refreshing the soul on a hot summer day. It's passing deluge an invitation to dance and revel in a momentary lapse back into childhood and pure joy. My arms fluttered in a frenzy of excited motion as we were all ushered into the ecstasy of the finale. Beads of perspiration glimmered off Blake's brow as he poured his heart out to his audience of One while performing to the thousands in the hall. The felt presence of something unearthly seemed to revel and dance within the pulse and measure of every note. This was the sound of heaven permeating the divide.

With the force like a peal of thunder, the final note echoed through the hall and resonated in a crescendo of harmony mixed with the roar of elated applause. The audience soared to their feet. Their ovation outlasted any other previously bestowed upon the Philharmonic. The accolades lingered well past the prolonged bows from myself and the orchestra. Both Alfie and Kyle were at my side in stunned silence as waves of applause and appreciation battered center stage where we stood.

I strained upwards hoping to meet Jessie's eye once again but she remained sitting, her eyes down and focused. A tear rolled down her cheek catching the light and emitting a momentary flicker as though it were a crystal from the lining on her dress. She had opened my letter and was reading it.

I closed my eyes and could see the words I wrote inside. A natural outflow from a healing heart as pure as the glacier stream rippling past my tree in heaven which I knew was growing once again.

Jessie,

I didn't know what love was for most of my life. I was afraid I would lose what little control I had left if I ever let my guard down long enough to let it in. Love pursued me and I ran, hiding behind the façade of my music which has been my life as well as the cave where I hid, shutting the rest of the world out.

I had nothing to give when I met you. I used you like I used music, determined to take and control instead of serve and surrender. But I know now that music and you are the most precious gifts in the world to me and can never be controlled or tamed.

It's taken a walk through the valley of the shadows to truly learn how to live. I had to almost lose my life in order that I might find it, and His love is now at the center of it all.

We have both known fathers in this world and to think on them is to invite memories of grief, abandonment, and pain. But I have met a Father who will never hurt us or abandon us. There is kindness in His eyes and healing in His embrace. He is an eternal song of hope and His love is a promise of rest for our weary souls. He is the beauty we gain in exchange for a handful of ashes. He is eternal life in exchange for hopelessness and death.

Jessie, if you will have me, I will make you this promise today: to love you for the rest of my life, holding you within the embrace of heaven's song, while the Father sings it over us.

I made him a promise while we walked together on a path suspended somewhere between heaven and earth. He asked me to give you a message. These are the words from his own heart he has wanted you to hear for a long time.

Jessie,

I've known you before your beginning. I was with you before you were born. I have loved you always and have never left you. I have been singing over you a song which is yours alone and it will never end.

There is a tree in heaven which I planted the day you were born. Though the world has tried to cut it down, it will never be removed from the deep roots of my love, which are its foundation. I was cut down so you could live and grow within me and now, nothing will ever separate us.

Why do you try and reconcile my existence with that of pain as though one cannot exist without the other? In this life there will be trouble. I myself know what it is to grieve, to suffer, and to die. I gave my life in the greatest exchange of all, to restore to you all that was broken and lost so that instead of sadness, you could know joy. Instead of distress, you could know peace. Instead of ashes, you could be clothed in my beauty.

Jessie, I have seen your tears and held you through your darkest sorrow. My tears mixed with yours as they fell. But though your heart has been broken, I will restore it. Though the sound of my song has grown faint in your ears, you will hear its melody once again.

Come to me with your broken heart, and I will make it new. Lie down and rest within the rhythm of my grace and the refrain of my song and know that you are loved.

You are loved.

You are loved.

Jessie's tears fell upon the letter in drops, each one expanding as they soaked into the paper. Her dark night of the soul was starting to dissipate in the morning rays of hope and healing rising in her heart.

My interview with Paul Waverley from *Vanity Fair* had resumed earlier that day back in my office. We settled into the same seats across from one another and talked into the digital recorder, picking up from where our conversation had ended so abruptly on the day of my collapse.

"Well, Michael, the last time we sat across from each other I was asking you about your inspiration. Do you think we can pull back the music this time and get to the man behind it?" He crossed his checkered slacks and placed on his knee a light blue straw fedora touting a bright red feather.

"That's going to be quite the conversation," I said. "I'm just beginning to get to know him myself."

"That's interesting." Paul raised an eyebrow as he said it. "What have you found out so far?"

"Well, for starters, I do believe in God." I sat forward in my chair and moved in, leaning my arms on my desk. My next words were on my tongue, but my eyes were pulled to the side, caught by images crowding my periphery.

The collection of framed pictures lining my desk had grown over the last number of weeks and the smiling faces now staring back at me could still pull at my heart with a glance. There was a new family photo with my mom and sisters as we stood together on Bow Bridge in Central Park—all of us closer than we have ever been as a family. Next to that, a wide frame held the photo of Travis Bishop and me standing side by side while residents of the East Baltimore Street Mission crowded around us like shimmers from gold in the bottom of a mining pan.

In another, Alfie and I stood side by side with Gloria and the three kids gathered in front, their eyes brimming with animated joy as we stood in front of their new home together on the day they received the keys. Next to that was a picture which had been taken during my hospital recovery. It was of me sitting up in my bed with Kate and Kyle leaning in on either side; Kyle's guitar rested across my lap. Kyle had just told me a few days ago he had placed a deposit on a ring. There was no question in his mind—she was the one.

And then there was Jessie's photo, the one from our honeymoon which had been there for the longest. The love I felt for her, at times, felt like an expanding ocean distending the borders of my heart—an unexplainable phenomenon kindled by a heavenly exchange. To me, that was the miracle and evidence of God, even more tangible than a return from the precipice of death.

"Paul, how much time do you have?" I asked with a grin. He returned a smile in silent response as if to welcome the journey laid out before us.

I told him about singing trees and broken hearts—shattered faith colliding with heaven's song in a symphony of redemption and love. The movement of my life had been one of retreat, driven into isolation by anger and pain. But a relentless love pursued me like the sun chasing away the night, and now the man I was becoming could finally step out from behind the music and tell his story.

When the crowds dispersed after the concert ended and the hall sat quiet once again, I found Jessie back in her private room where the floral scent still hung like a soft sustain in a ballad. Her eyes were still red and her makeup smudged, but I had never taken in a more beautiful sight. No words were exchanged as we embraced and cried in each other's arms. We lost all sense of time while the moment passed like a spring rain soaking into parched land.

Eventually, after a catharsis of tears, talking and laughter, we walked out of David Geffen Hall hand in hand into a new day and a new life together.

THE END

Epilogue and Author's Note: A Ship Called Destiny

This book would not have been written without this narrative, which came in the form of a dream one morning. A morning where I was at a low point and couldn't see my way forward. The evening before I had crawled under my bedcovers well before bedtime, exhausted from the despair brought about by a discouraging day. My failures as a father—moments when I chose abrupt rebuke because I couldn't find patient correction—were now playing in a loop through my mind.

"Father," I wept in a whisper, muffled by my bedcovers, "how am I supposed to be a father to the fatherless, a desire you've placed in my heart, when I can't seem to get it right with my own kids?" Such was my state the night before.

The next morning I woke up to the very presence of Father God himself filling my bedroom—peace with weight. It was like waking up in another reality where you couldn't access the failures and despair of your past for the overwhelming and tangible grace enveloping me. He spoke to me as soon as I woke up: "I'm still going to use you." These were the words that filled my heart and rolled through my mind, replacing my loop of failures. I didn't say anything back and just lay captivated in the moment until falling back to sleep. That's when I had this dream.

We've all experienced low points in life where it feels as though we are watching distance grow between us and our dreams, like a ship shrinking into an elusive horizon. We've all been tempted to embrace despair. But that is not the story the Father has written for you. So stand there, on the docks and wait. It won't be long before you hear his invitation—he speaks it over you every day. Why? Because he's a good Captain and he wants you with him in this great adventure we call life.

This short story was my first foray into writing. I hope you enjoy it.

I stood and watched as the large ship distanced itself from the dock where I stood. Though I could have hit it with a stone, the open water parting it from me might as well have been an ocean. And though it was no longer tied to land, it pulled at my heart as it moved farther away, as though I was attached to it with an invisible string. All I could do was watch it move further and feel my heart ache. You see, that was my ship and I wasn't supposed to miss it. It was the only one and I knew there wouldn't be another. I could still make out the name as it turned its bow towards open water and away from me. The ship's name was "Destiny."

I felt helpless. All I could do was stand and watch, like a runner who's stumbled before the finish line in a race he knew he was supposed to win. I don't know how long I stood there for before I heard a rusty voice behind me.

"Would you like to join me on my ship, son?"

I turned to see an old sailor with a white beard holding a lit pipe in his hands. His skin was weathered and his eyes were piercing but kind. He wore a tattered navy blue jacket and a grey tweed cap. With his pipe he indicated towards his vessel tied at the end of the dock. I hadn't noticed it there before. I don't think I could have hidden my disappointment as I looked upon what he called his "ship." Actually, to call it anything more than a dinghy would have been kind. But not wanting to insult the kind stranger, and not having any other option or thought in mind in that moment, I accepted his offer and boarded his boat.

As we broke away from the dock, the sailor made no conversation and I was left alone with my thoughts. I hadn't bothered to see if the sailor's vessel had a name but as we continued on I began to think of names that now seemed fitting for my journey. Disappointment. Disqualified. Despair.

I didn't bother to look up as we drifted along, but my misery was interrupted as our boat began to rock in some waves. Looking up I saw once again my ship getting closer, as the sailor seemed to be coursing straight for it. Our little boat was being tossed in Destiny's wake.

I couldn't make a sound, though a thousand questions began to clamor in my mind. It was all happening so fast and the sailor seemed to know what he was doing. Just before I thought we would collide into the hull of my ship, the sailor piloted us alongside and stopped. A rope ladder dropped down before us and he began climbing. "Follow me," he said without turning his head back at me. Again, more questions assailed my mind, but none of them found my voice. Instead, I grabbed hold of the ladder and climbed.

Seeing for the first time Destiny's deck was more glorious than I had ever imagined, but it wasn't the sight of the ship itself that took my breath away. I was expecting to see the ship's crew busying themselves about their tasks, too occupied to notice two disheveled castaways join their number; instead, I was looking out over the orderly columns and rows of the entire ship's crew standing at attention. All was silent except for the flag on Destiny's mast snapping in the wind. It was a reverent sight to behold. At the exact spot where we had climbed on board, there was a straight aisle cut through the ranks of men leading to the center of the ship. The old sailor approached one of the crew standing at the front of the line and handed him his jacket and cap. Just then, two other crewmen approached carrying a uniform. One held a white jacket decorated with fine tassels and medals. The other carried a regal captain's hat. The old sailor put them on and a loud voice bellowed, "Captain on deck!"

With the sound like a thunder clap, the entire company of sailors, in a unified response, stomped their right feet as they stood again at attention and raised their hands in salute. Then the old man sailor — the Captain of my Destiny — looked at me with a smile and a wink and then turned back and addressed the crew. "Gentlemen, I have a guest. He belongs here with us and with me. I expect you all to extend to him the same level of honor you show to me." He then turned back to me and extended his hand, "Come with me, son." We walked past the rows of crew, while they maintained their salute, towards the helm of Destiny. And as we walked, though I didn't turn back to see, I could imagine that a little dinghy I called 'despair' was slowly drifting away.

Manufactured by Amazon.ca
Bolton, ON

13088548R00146